How could I choose?

"Kate, it's a good thing you won six tickets to Wilderness World in the raffle, so we can all go!" Stephanie said. She, Patti, and I all jumped up and down.

"But wait — six isn't enough, Steph," Lauren interrupted our celebration. "It's only enough for Mr. and Mrs. Beekman, Kate, Melissa, and two other Sleepover Friends." We all stopped and stared at each other.

I could hardly face Patti, Lauren, and Stephanie. How could I tell one of them she couldn't come to Wilderness World? How could I possibly choose?

Look for these and other books
in the Sleepover Friends Series:

Super Sleepover Guide

Kate the Winner!

Susan Saunders

AN
APPLE
PAPERBACK

SCHOLASTIC INC.
New York Toronto London Auckland Sydney

ISBN 0-590-43925-1

12 11 10 9 8 7 6 5 4 3 2 1   1 2 3 4 5 6/9

Printed in the U.S.A.   28

First Scholastic printing, March 1991

Chapter
1

"Let's go to Just Juniors first," Stephanie Green suggested as she led us through the main entrance of the mall. "I want to try on the black-and-red-striped miniskirt I've been talking about."

Just Juniors is one of our favorite clothes stores. It was a typical Tuesday afternoon in Riverhurst, and I was browsing with my friends Patti Jenkins, Stephanie, and Lauren Hunter at the mall after school.

I'm Kate Beekman, and the four of us are almost always together. We're in the same fifth-grade class at Riverhurst Elementary. Plus we spend most of our time after school and on the weekends together, not to mention the fact that we have sleepovers together almost every Friday night. We call ourselves the Sleepover Friends.

"Why don't we stop by Sweet Stuff since it's on

our way," Patti suggested. "I've been thinking about white chocolate bark all day."

"Okay," Lauren agreed. "I'll get some nuts or something. I'm pretty hungry."

"*You're* hungry?" I said, and Patti and Stephanie laughed. I can't help it. I like to give Lauren a hard time about her appetite. She knows I'm only teasing. Plus, she admits that she eats more than the average eleven-year-old. Good thing she doesn't gain weight.

A little while ago, Lauren had three cavities filled, and she hated it so much that she's gone on a health food kick. I've been waiting for it to wear off, but it hasn't yet. I tried to eat healthy stuff, too, but I only lasted about two weeks!

"Come on, you guys, speed up. It took me a week to convince my parents to give me next month's allowance early," Stephanie said. "I'm afraid the skirt will be gone if I wait another minute."

If Lauren's love is food, Stephanie's is clothing. She already has her own style of dressing — always in black, red, and white, which looks great with her dark, curly hair. She pays a lot more attention to fashion trends and stuff than I do.

"Patti, why don't you and Lauren go to Sweet Stuff while Steph and I go to Just Juniors?" I suggested. "I might try on a couple of shirts or something. You can just meet us there." (Okay, I confess.

I like to organize. But *someone* has to keep these guys together!)

"Want us to get you anything?" Patti asked.

"Get me the usual," I told her. Sweet Stuff has the best candy in Riverhurst. Everything they sell is really good, but we each have a favorite. Mine is Gummi Bears.

"You, too, Stephanie?" Lauren asked.

"No, I'll need all of my money for the skirt. Besides, if I want it to look good on me, I can't be eating candy." Stephanie puffed her cheeks out. See what I mean? What fifth-grader do you know who worries so much about her looks?

"Okay, see ya," Lauren said as she and Patti turned around and started walking back toward Sweet Stuff. Then Lauren suddenly spun back around. "Hey! Isn't that Cub Scout over there Nancy Hersh's little brother Brian?" She pointed toward the huge fountain in the center of the mall.

Nancy Hersh is in 5B with us. Her brother Brian is only six, but we know him because he used to be in Patti's little brother Horace's first-grade class. Horace skipped into second grade a while ago, but that's another story.

I couldn't really see who Lauren was talking about until we walked closer — I'm nearsighted. The only time I wear my glasses in public, though, is if

I'm at a movie. I love movies and don't like to miss *anything*. When I get older, I'm going to be a famous director.

"Let's see what's going on," Patti said.

I followed Lauren, Stephanie, and Patti to the fountain. As we got closer, I could see five boys in Cub Scout uniforms standing behind a booth.

"Hi, Brian," Patti said. "What's going on?"

Brian hung his head shyly. "We're selling raffle tickets," he explained. "My mom dropped us off after school. But I left the poster that lists all the great prizes in her car." Brian looked like he was about to start crying.

Patti, who's the nicest person I know, couldn't stand to see him looking so sad. "We'll each buy one," she volunteered. "How much do they cost?"

"One dollar each," he beamed.

"We'll take four," Patti said. We each gave Brian a dollar and filled out our ticket stubs. Patti added, "If we see anyone else from school here, we'll send them over to the booth."

"Thanks a lot!" Brian said happily. His mood had really improved. "Don't forget: You have to be here for the drawing at nine o'clock Friday night to win."

Stephanie looked at her watch. (It's red, with black hands, and doesn't have any numbers.) "Speaking of time, I *have* to get to Just Juniors," she

4

reminded us. "Come on, Kate." She grabbed my arm and dragged me a couple of feet while Patti and Lauren headed off toward Sweet Stuff.

I managed to pry my arm out of Stephanie's Hulk Hogan grip.

"We forgot to ask Brian what the raffle prizes are," I said as I massaged my red wrist.

"It doesn't matter," Stephanie said. "We won't win anyway."

"I know," I agreed. "But I felt sorry for him."

"Me, too," Stephanie said absently as she made a beeline to the rack of skirts. She tried on the black-and-red-striped miniskirt with a red sweater. I found a blue vest and a pair of black stirrup pants that I liked, so I took them into the dressing room.

Patti and Lauren finally came to meet us, holding their Sweet Stuff bags. Lauren, former Snack Queen of Riverhurst, had a bag of dried apple slices! Talk about boring!

Stephanie and I had finished looking, so we got in line to pay for our things. Stephanie got her skirt, of course, and I had decided to get the blue vest.

After Just Juniors, we still had an hour before Lauren's brother Roger was supposed to pick us up. He's seventeen and has his own car. He's pretty nice, and gives us rides sometimes when we don't want to ride our bikes.

I reached into my bag of candy. Give me Gummi

5

Bears over dried apple slices any day! "Let's go look at the fish at Feathers and Fins," I said. Feathers and Fins is a pet store that has aquariums stacked along its walls. They have all kinds of neat, weird fish, plus lots of exotic birds.

After Feathers and Fins we went to the Record Emporium and listened to the latest Hypnosis album on headphones. Ellen Meadows, Hypnosis's lead singer, is my favorite female rock star.

We window-shopped a little more at Playing Around and Ceramica. "Oh, no!" Lauren suddenly shouted. "Roger's gonna be here in two minutes. And we have to get all the way to the other end of the mall!" Roger's nice, but he doesn't like to have to wait for us. I can't blame him. Roger's had to put up with a lot from the Sleepover Friends — for a long time!

In kindergarten, it was just me and Lauren. We lived only one house apart on Pine Street. (Now the Hunters live almost two miles away, on Brio Drive.) Eventually, we started taking turns sleeping over at each other's house on the weekends. My dad called us the Sleepover Twins, even though we don't look alike at all! I'm short, with blonde hair, and Lauren is tall and thin, with brown hair.

Then Stephanie moved from the city to the other end of Pine Street. She was in Mr. Civello's fourth-grade class with Lauren, and Lauren thought Stephanie was a lot of fun, so she invited her to one of our sleepovers. As far as I was concerned, Stephanie made a *horrible* first impression! But after I got used to her, I decided Stephanie was actually kind of neat. Since Sleepover Twins didn't apply anymore, my dad decided to call us the Sleepover Trio.

That didn't last long, though. At the beginning of the year, Patti showed up in Mrs. Mead's class. She's tall, with brown hair, and is *really* smart. She and Stephanie had known each other in the city, and Lauren and I both liked her right away. Now my dad calls us the Sleepover Friends! That ought to last a long time.

Lauren and Patti raced ahead to the mall exit. They have long legs, so they run faster than Stephanie and I do. We finally caught up with them right at the front doors. And just in time! Roger pulled up right as we pushed the huge glass doors open.

That Friday, the sleepover was at my house. My parents had offered to take us to a movie before the official sleepover began. Kevin DeSpain's new movie, *Endlessly,* had just opened at the mall. Kevin DeSpain is the star of our favorite TV show, *Made for Each Other.*

Kevin DeSpain is absolutely the worst actor. Patti, Lauren, and Stephanie think he's really cute. We all actually got to meet him once at Patti's house, and he *was* good-looking *and* nice. But I still don't think a person's a good actor just because he's adorable.

As soon as Lauren, Patti, and Stephanie had arrived, my father said, "Okay, everybody, let's go! Everyone in the car."

"We're not all going to fit in your car, Dad," I pointed out. "Or Mom's, for that matter."

"She's right, Morris," my mother said. "Maybe we should think about getting a station wagon or a minivan."

"But we only have two children," Dad said. I have one sister, Melissa, who's in third grade. I think she's finally starting to become human. She used to be so awful I called her Melissa the Monster.

"Yes, but we also have their friends," Mom said and smiled at us. Patti, Stephanie, Lauren, and I grinned.

So we piled into both my parents' cars. My mother took Patti and Lauren and Melissa with her; Dad drove me and Stephanie.

Once we were at the mall, my parents got on line to buy our tickets to *Endlessly*. As they handed us each a ticket, my mother said, "We've decided that you can sit by yourselves tonight."

"Yay!" we all cheered — including Melissa. She usually tries to get in on our Sleepover Friends business.

"Me-lis-sa," I pleaded. "Can't you sit with Mom and Dad tonight?" I knew she wouldn't like it if I *told* her what to do, so I tried to make it sound like I was asking.

Melissa put her hand on her hip. "Uh-uh. Ask Mom," she said.

I looked up at my mother with a pleading expression.

"Melissa, I think it would be best if we let the girls watch the movie by themselves. We can have a Beekman party together, with just us," she explained.

"Well, okay," Melissa said.

Patti, Stephanie, Lauren, and I breathed a sigh of relief. Melissa seemed satisfied, too. As we walked into the theater, we heard her say, "And we'll have a Beekman popcorn and Beekman Coke and . . ."

The movie was okay — not great. I thought the photography was sloppy, and some of the music was really wrong for the mood they were trying to create. But maybe I have higher standards than my friends do.

"Weren't the costumes absolutely magnificent?" Stephanie asked as we were walking toward the mall exit doors.

"And Kevin DeSpain!" Patti and Lauren said at the same time.

"Give me a br — " I began.

"Kate Beekman." My name suddenly filled the mall! "Kate Beekman is our first-place winner," a voice continued. I stopped dead in my tracks. For the first time, I noticed a crowd of people gathered around the fountain in the middle of the mall. Lauren had stopped so suddenly that the popcorn she was holding flew out of the box! And Patti and Stephanie just stood there like they were statues. I stared at my friends with wide eyes. What was going on?

"Honey?" my mom said uncertainly.

"Is Kate Beekman here?" the voice boomed. "Kate Beekman?" Then I saw that the voice was coming from a man in a scoutmaster uniform. Oh my gosh — the raffle!

"The raffle," I said weakly. I tried to say, "I'm here!" but the words got caught in my dry throat.

Melissa took charge. "She's here!" she screamed at the top of her voice. "She's right here!" For once, I was glad that Melissa was around, and that she had such a piercing yell!

Then Lauren grabbed my arm and dragged me through the crowd to the man behind the microphone. He shook my hand. "Congratulations, Kate," he said. "I'm Mr. Reynolds."

Cameras flashed in my face and practically blinded me. I probably looked like a deer caught in someone's headlights! I was still completely in shock.

Then a woman from the *Riverhurst Clarion* started asking me questions. "How old are you? Where do you go to school? Where do you live?" She scribbled my responses in her notebook.

As I came back to reality, I realized I didn't even know what I'd won. "What's my prize?" I asked Mr. Reynolds. I started to get a grip on myself — after all, it was probably a toaster or something.

"You've won six, four-day passes to Wilderness World, with free lodging and admission to the park!" Wilderness World! I got excited again!

Wilderness World is an amusement park that's about a five-hour drive from Riverhurst. Everything in the park relates to its wilderness theme. I had been wanting to go there forever! My parents, Melissa, and the Sleepover Friends all crowded around me as Mr. Reynolds shook my hand again.

"I can't believe it, Kate!" Lauren cried. "I'd completely forgotten about the raffle!"

"If the movie had let out just five minutes later," Patti said wonderingly, "you wouldn't have won."

Just then, I noticed that two of my least-favorite people, Ginger Kinkaid and Christy Soames, were standing at the edge of the crowd that had gathered for the raffle. They're both in 5C and they're inseparable. "Oooh! Wilderness World!" Ginger mimicked us in a high-pitched voice. Then she added, in her normal voice, "How babyish."

11

"You're just jealous, Vir-gin-ia!" Lauren said back. Ginger hates her real name. I'd never heard Lauren call her that to her face!

"Hardly," Ginger replied. "Christy's dad is taking Christy and me on vacation for spring break. I'm sure we'll go somewhere much cooler than Wilderness World. And it *won't* be crawling with preschoolers." She and Christy sauntered away.

"Who do they think they are?" Stephanie fumed. I was too angry to say anything.

"They're just jealous," Patti said. "I bet they entered the raffle, too, but lost."

"Patti's right," Lauren said. "They wouldn't know how to have fun anyway." By now the crowd had gone and the Scouts had packed up their stuff. Mr. Reynolds had given a pamphlet to my Dad that explained how I could pick up the tickets.

Just then my mother spoke up. "Morris, maybe the whole family and the Sleepover Friends could all go to Wilderness World over the girls' spring break," she suggested.

"Sure. I'll see if I can get someone to fill in for me at the hospital," Dad said. He's a doctor at Central County Hospital, and my mom works there as a volunteer.

I perked up and practically forgot all about the icky scene with Ginger and Christy. "It's a good thing you won six tickets so we can all go!" Stephanie said. She, Patti, and I all jumped up and down.

"But wait — six *isn't* enough, Steph," Lauren interrupted our celebration. "It's only enough for Mr. and Mrs. Beekman, Kate, Melissa, and *two* other Sleepover Friends." We all stopped and stared at each other. Melissa looked worried for a second, then realized there was no way she would be left behind. Now I really *did* forget all about Ginger and Christy. *This* problem was much bigger!

I could hardly face Patti, Lauren, and Stephanie. How could I tell one of them she couldn't come to Wilderness World? How could I possibly choose?

"Well! There's plenty of time to talk about this later, girls," Mom said quickly. "Who wants to stop at Charlie's and pick up a carton of double Dutch chocolate ice cream on the way home?"

"And hot fudge topping?" Stephanie asked. So much for worrying about how that miniskirt would look!

Mom smiled. "*And* whipped cream," she promised.

Chapter
2

At the sleepover that night, no one wanted to put any pressure on me to make a decision about which Sleepover Friends would be invited to join my family at Wilderness World. But it was obvious that it was on everyone's mind.

Lauren tried to talk about something else. "Did you hear Jenny Carlin at lunch today? She kept telling everyone how her parents are taking her to Hawaii over spring break,"she said. Jenny Carlin is in 5B — unfortunately. She's always showing off about something.

"Yeah. And Angela Kemp's going with them," Stephanie said.

"Great! Two of my favorite people," Lauren said sarcastically. Angela is Jenny's best friend. Actually, she's more like a sidekick. Wherever Jenny goes and whatever Jenny does, Angela's there, obeying Jenny's every request.

But I didn't care what Jenny Carlin was doing for vacation. All I could think about was *my* vacation — which I wanted to spend with the Sleepover Friends. *All* of them. I kept wishing I'd get a call saying they'd forgotten to give me my seventh ticket! I was getting pretty down, and suddenly I wanted to be alone. "Um . . . I'm going to get some more . . . Dr Pepper," I said.

"I'll help you," Lauren volunteered.

"No, that's okay," I said. "I'll just bring the bottle up. I can get it myself." I left quickly before anyone could tell how upset I was.

Downstairs, I grabbed a two-liter bottle of soda from the fridge. Maybe Dad wouldn't take time off for Wilderness World. After all, his patients need him. That didn't really seem fair, though. He definitely deserved a vacation. Besides, if it hadn't been for him and Mom, I never would have been there to win in the first place. *I'd really like to leave Melissa the Monster behind.* But I knew that wasn't right, either. Mom and Dad had already promised she could go. I almost wished I hadn't won at all!

I tried to think of ways to choose who would go to Wilderness World. Draw straws? Have some kind of contest? This was the most horrible decision I'd ever had to make. I mean, I had known Lauren the longest — I thought of her as my oldest and best friend. But how could I choose between Patti and Stephanie? No matter who I picked, someone would end up sad — and probably mad at me. What I really needed was to find a way so that *all* the Sleepover Friends could go.

As I walked back to my room, I heard Stephanie, Patti, and Lauren talking about the Wilderness World trip. I guess they didn't hear me coming.

"Poor Kate," Patti whispered. "It must be really hard for her to decide which two of us to take. I know *I'd* have a hard time."

Stephanie was a little less understanding. "I don't see what's so hard about it," she said. "She should just pick. Whoever isn't chosen will understand." I wasn't as sure of that as Stephanie was!

I felt guilty about listening at the door, so I pushed it open and pretended I hadn't heard a thing. "Who wants more Dr Pepper?" I asked casually, my voice cracking a little.

"We've been talking about Wilderness World, Kate," Lauren said. Now I felt *really* guilty. Then Lauren's eyes opened up as if a light bulb had gone off in her head. "I have an idea!" she said. "Maybe our parents will pay for one of us to go. Then no one will get left out."

"That's a great idea," I told her, sighing with relief. For once, Lauren had put her imagination on hold and come up with a practical way to solve the problem!

"We'll all ask our parents this weekend," Stephanie said. "I know my folks will let me go." Stephanie *does* usually get what she wants — probably because for a long time she was an only child. Now she has a twin baby brother and sister named Jeremy and Emma. But I guess her parents got used to Stephanie getting her way, because most of the time she still does. We don't mind, though, because Stephanie usually shares whatever she gets!

"It's worth a try," Patti said, perking up.

Now that we had figured out the solution to our Wilderness World crisis, we could get on with our sleepover. "Who's ready for some Mad Libs?" I asked, pulling the Mad Lib pad out of my desk drawer.

Patti, Lauren, and Stephanie all yelled, "Me!"

I flipped to the first unused page. "Plural noun," I read.

"Best friends," Lauren said matter-of-factly, and grinned.

Monday before school, I pedaled my bike to the corner of Hillcrest and Pine to meet the others.

I hadn't spoken to anyone since our Belgian waffle breakfast Saturday morning. Patti's parents had taken her and Horace to an out-of-town history conference. Mr. and Mrs. Jenkins both teach at the university in Riverhurst. Lauren had gone to visit her grandmother in Bellvale. And Stephanie's parents had friends from the city visiting all weekend, so Stephanie had to stick around to help out with Emma and Jeremy.

I hadn't been able to concentrate all morning — I'd been worrying about whether anyone's parents would pay for the extra ticket. By the time I got to the corner, Patti and Stephanie were already waiting for me, and I was ready to explode!

"We were about to leave without you," Stephanie said. "We figured you weren't coming. You're never late."

I looked at my watch. "I had trouble getting up this morning," I explained. "I hardly slept last night."

We waited another minute for Lauren, then we really had to go or we'd be late. I knew she would whiz into class about three seconds before the late bell rang.

As we rode along, everyone made small talk about the weekend. We were almost halfway to school when I couldn't take the suspense any longer. "So? Did your parents agree to pay for your ticket to Wilderness World, or what?" I asked.

From the way they looked at each other, I could tell that they had already discussed it. I could also tell it wasn't good news. Patti couldn't even look at me.

"My parents reminded me that they had already advanced me next month's allowance to pay for that new miniskirt," Stephanie apologized.

"Mine can't give me the money, either," Patti said softly. "It's not my birthday or anything."

"Did anyone talk to Lauren this weekend?" I asked. They shook their heads. "Well, maybe *her* parents will give her the money. Then our problem will be solved." I tried to look calm, but I was pretty worried. I didn't see how Mr. and Mrs. Hunter could give Lauren almost ninety dollars, which is how much a four-day pass to Wilderness World costs. I guess it had been a dumb idea after all.

Lauren was standing in front of the bike rack when we rode up to our school. "Any luck with your parents?" she called as we hopped off our bikes.

"None," Patti, Stephanie, and I said together.

"Me, neither."

There wasn't time to talk about Wilderness World anymore before school. If you're tardy twice, you have to sit in Principal Wainwright's office during lunch, plus write an essay about the importance of getting to school on time. Yuck!

We slipped into our seats just as the late bell rang.

"Cutting it close, girls," Mrs. Mead warned us.

We didn't have a chance to speak to each other the rest of the morning. But during our social studies filmstrip, Stephanie managed to pass me a note that said, *I've thought of a way we can ALL go to Wilderness World!*

I tried not to get too excited, but I couldn't wait to find out her plan. I was so desperate, I was willing to try anything.

After what seemed like an entire week, Mrs. Mead dismissed us for lunch. We all filed through the lunch line, loaded up our trays, and sat down at our usual table. "Well? Spill it! What's the plan?"

"What plan?" Lauren asked.

"The plan to get us all to Wilderness World." Stephanie poked at her mashed potatoes and leaned forward. "Whoever Kate decides is the extra guest will *earn* the money by getting jobs around Riverhurst!"

I got hopeful. It *could* work. But Patti frowned. "Why don't we *all* work to try to raise enough money to pay for one ticket? That way, Kate doesn't have to decide which two of us to take." Good old Patti!

Lauren stopped eating her lima beans. "And with all of us working together," she said, "we can earn the money in practically no time!"

Just then, Larry Jackson and Mark Freedman sat down next to us. They're in Mrs. Mead's class, too, and they go everywhere together. "Way to go, Beekman," Mark congratulated me.

"I hear you won passes to Wilderness World," Larry said as he opened his milk carton. "All right!"

"Yeah," Mark said. "I bought ten raffle tickets and didn't win anything."

Christy and Ginger were sitting right behind us at the next table, so they could hear everything. Just my luck. "Gee," Ginger said sarcastically, "I wish I could scrub floors for a week so I could go to a baby-fied amusement park and be bored out of my mind."

"The wicked witch of the west strikes again," Stephanie murmured under her breath.

As if it weren't bad enough having Ginger and Christy nearby, Taylor Sprouse sauntered past our table. He's a sixth-grader, and the most conceited boy in school. I've never seen anyone fuss with their hair so much — not even Stephanie!

"Hey, girls," he taunted. "I hear Wilderness World is so stupid, they have to *give* the tickets away."

"But Taylor," one of his friends said, "you entered that raffle, too." We all practically rolled on the floor, laughing. Taylor turned beet red and sat at a table on the other side of the cafeteria. Sleepover Friends: one; Taylor Sprouse: zero!

* * *

21

That night, the phone rang during *The Wackiest Videos Ever*. It's on every night at seven o'clock. Melissa hopped up from the couch and raced to the kitchen. "I got it!" she yelled, even though my dad was only about two feet away from her, cleaning up after dinner. After she said "Hello," there was a pause and then she yelled, "Kaaaaate! It's for you!"

I slid out of the recliner and scooted around the corner. "Thanks. I almost didn't hear you," I said sarcastically. She stuck her tongue out and skipped back to her seat. Did I say she was almost human? She has a way to go. "Hello?" I said.

"It's all set, Kate," Lauren said, sounding like she was eating a carrot stick or something. "We all asked our parents, and they said it's okay with them if we try to earn money for the extra pass." Crunch, crunch.

"All right!" My troubles were over! No more worrying about picking the top two Sleepover Friends!

"Mrs. Jenkins and Mr. Green are going to call your parents to make sure they don't have any problems with our plan," Lauren explained. "And my mom wants to talk to yours when we're through."

We talked a little while about what a pain Christy and Ginger are, and how dopey Taylor Sprouse is. When we finished, I said, "Mom, Mrs. Hunter wants to talk to you." She took the phone from me with a puzzled look on her face.

I sat on a stool and listened. "Hi, Ann," Mom said, smiling. "How's the new neighborhood? Well, we really miss you, too. It's just not the same after all these years." I couldn't take the small talk much longer. I perked up when I heard Mom say, "Of course, we'd love to take the girls to Wilderness World. I'm glad they're being so industrious about finding a way for everyone to go." Great! I motioned to my mother to give me back the phone. "I think the girls want to talk again, Ann," she said. "Okay . . . bye."

"Lauren, can you get Roger to drive you over?" I asked as soon as my mother handed me the phone. "I'm calling an emergency Sleepover Friends meeting. We'd better start making plans *immediately*."

"Sure," Lauren said, still munching away. "I'll call Stephanie, and you call Patti."

"Right."

Stephanie showed up about ten minutes later. Her father called right before she rang the doorbell. Of course, my mother told him our plan was fine with her and Dad. And Mrs. Jenkins came to the door with Patti. Once again, Mom explained that she thought our idea was great. "I know we'll all have a wonderful time," she said.

23

Roger dropped Lauren off. Even though we were inside the house, we could hear Roger saying, "Not one minute after nine o'clock."

"I know, I know," Lauren said.

We all raced up the stairs to my bedroom. "It looks like your plan is actually going to work, Stephanie." I could barely sit still.

"Did you doubt me for a moment?" she said jokingly.

"Now, what will the three of us do to earn the money?" Patti asked. "It's just one ticket, but it still costs a lot."

"The three of you?" I said. "We're all in this together. I want to help out, too."

"Way to go, Kate," Lauren said and punched me in the arm. I fell to the floor and pretended like she'd really done some damage.

"But what jobs should we get?" Stephanie asked. "I don't think Alice and Bernice need part-time helpers anymore." Alice and Bernice own an antique store, and Stephanie and Lauren used to work there a few afternoons a week. That's where Lauren got her cool bed.

"Why don't we throw a couple of birthday parties?" Lauren suggested. We have a party service for the little kids in Riverhurst. Lauren dresses up like a dog, Barkly, and Patti dresses up kind of like a fairy, Sparkly, and Stephanie and I videotape everything.

24

"Unfortunately, we don't know anyone who's going to have a birthday before spring break," Patti reminded us. "And we still have to use our party money to pay off the camera." When we got the video camera, we couldn't afford to buy it outright, so we pay off a little each month.

"Patti's right. But we don't have to decide tonight. I think we should each come up with a list of four or five possible jobs," I said, "and we'll compare them tomorrow at lunch."

This was going to be my first good night's sleep since winning the tickets. With the four of us working together, earning that money should be a cinch. "Anyone for some of my mom's strawberry cheesecake?" I asked, even though I knew the answer. My mom and dad are both excellent cooks.

Lauren bit her lip. "Is there much sugar in that?" she asked. Patti, Stephanie, and I rolled our eyes.

"Lauren, you don't seem to understand," Stephanie said patiently. "We're talking about *cheesecake* here. How can you pass it up?"

"Oh, right, right," Lauren said, slapping her forehead. "What was I thinking of?" We all laughed as we filed down to the kitchen.

Chapter
3

We met at our usual table the next day at lunch. Taylor Sprouse was nowhere in sight. After yesterday's humiliation, he was probably too embarrassed to show up for school at all! Christy and Ginger were at the next table looking through travel brochures, but they were too busy figuring out where they wanted to spend spring break to worry about us.

"I'm so excited," Stephanie said, settling into her chair. "I've thought of so many neat things we can do to raise money."

"Just remember," I reminded them, "we only have two weeks. We have to narrow our lists down to jobs that can get us enough money — fast. Should we do one or two big jobs, or spread our effort over a lot of smaller jobs?"

Everyone thought awhile. Finally Patti said, "I think several small jobs would be better."

"Me, too," Lauren agreed.

"I want to get it over with as fast as possible," Stephanie objected. Stephanie does *not* like to sweat. "We raised a lot of money from that yard sale we had. That took us just one day."

Everyone looked at me. They were waiting for me to make a decision. I could either tie the vote up, or decide to go with Lauren and Patti. On the one hand, Stephanie was right. A while ago, Stephanie thought her father had lost his job. She was so worried about her parents that we had held an emergency yard sale. Stephanie even sold her favorite black leather jacket to Lauren. It turned out Mr. Green hadn't lost his job at all. Mrs. Green was pregnant with Emma and Jeremy! We *did* raise a lot of money from the sale. But it took us a long time to get everything ready, *and* a few other kids from Riverhurst Elementary had sold things, too, which attracted a lot of customers. "Smaller jobs," I said. Stephanie frowned. She perked up, though, when I said, "Why don't you read what's on your list, Steph?"

"Okay. Jewelry-making, fortune-telling, cooking lessons . . ." she began. Jewelry-making? Cooking lessons? And there was *absolutely* no way I was going to participate in something as ridiculous as fortune-telling. This was going to be tougher than I had thought. Lauren looked as worried as I did. Stephanie, who didn't notice our concerned glances, kept reading. "Delivery service, window-washing . . ."

"That's a good idea," I interrupted.

"What? Jewelry-making? Yeah, I th — "

"No, window-washing," I explained. "But you're the last person I expected to suggest housework."

"I know," Stephanie agreed. "But my parents pay a fortune to have someone wash our windows. I figure if we only do one or two houses, that's all the money we need." Patti and Lauren nodded, so I wrote it down in the notebook I'd brought along.

"Patti, what did you come up with?" I asked.

Patti suggested, "Dog-walking, used book sale, tutoring . . ." Patti's the class brain, so tutoring would be fine for her. But the rest of us could use tutoring ourselves! Her other ideas were good, but I wasn't sure they'd be very profitable.

"We need to think of things that *everyone* will enjoy doing," I said, trying not to sound too bossy.

"I did have one more idea, but it would take a lot of preparation," Patti explained. "We could have a bake sale here at school — if we got permission." I was a little surprised, since neither she nor her parents are very big on cooking. "It's cost-efficient and practical. And we'd probably have willing customers." Lauren ate a spoonful of orange Jell-O and nodded.

"Okay. That's two projects," I said and scribbled the idea underneath Stephanie's. "Lauren, let's hear what's on your list."

"I thought it would be a good idea to put on a circus with Fredericka, Cinders, Adelaide, and, of course, Rocky." Fredericka is my calico cat, which the Sleepover Friends got me for my birthday. Cinders belongs to Stephanie — she's completely black, of course. Adelaide is Patti's, and Lauren owns Rocky. They're all from the same litter. It sounded like fun, but Adelaide was the only kitten that was actually trained to do any tricks. Patti had trained her for a big science fair.

"I don't think Cinders knows there's more to life than eating and sleeping. The bigger she gets, the lazier she gets," Stephanie laughed. "You can count her out."

Lauren said thoughtfully, "Well, I do have a backup plan. How about dog-washing? Lots of kids at school have dogs — plus our neighbors." *What a great idea!* I thought. "We can do it on Saturday at my house. We'll advertise by putting up posters around school. We can start with Bullwinkle, of course." Bullwinkle is Roger's 130-pound black Newfoundland. He's seven years old, but still acts like a puppy. A *massive* puppy.

"Fortunately, you have a swimming pool to rinse him off in," Stephanie giggled.

29

Everyone seemed to like Lauren's idea, so I jotted *dog wash* in my notebook.

"So, Kate, what's on your list?" Lauren asked. As I looked it over, I could see that my own suggestions weren't very practical: *collect aluminum cans and return them for money, show videos at my house and charge admission* . . . Then I came to one that wasn't bad.

"Lots of people are working on their gardens now that it's spring. I bet we could do some yard work and make lots of money," I said.

Stephanie grabbed a french fry off my plate. "I think we've come up with four great ideas," she announced. "We'll be able to buy the extra ticket and have some spending money left over."

Whew! Thank goodness that went over well. Stephanie was right — everything was going very smoothly. We had four great projects, and nearly two whole weeks to earn the money. Wilderness World, get ready for the Sleepover Friends!

"Let's go to my house after school," Stephanie suggested. "I have poster board left over from last month's social studies project. We can use it to advertise the dog wash."

"I can only stay until about four-thirty," Lauren said. "Tonight's my night to make dinner." Both of Lauren's parents work full-time now, so Lauren and Roger share chores. Lauren doesn't exactly make dinner — her mother prepares it the night before and puts it in the freezer. Lauren pops it in the oven at the right time the next day.

"That's no problem. We can finish up tomorrow," Stephanie assured her.

"Who's going to ask Mrs. Wainwright if it's okay for us to hang the posters?" I said, looking at the others.

"*And* have the bake sale?" Lauren added.

We all just looked at each other for what seemed like an hour. "I'll . . . do it," Patti finally spoke up. "The bake sale was my idea."

Lauren gave in, too. "But the dog wash was mine," she said. "I'll go with you."

"We'll all go," I said, looking directly at Stephanie. "The money's for all of us."

Stephanie snatched another fry. "Right!" she nodded as she bit it in half.

Mrs. Wainwright always stands in the lobby after school, so after our last class we knew where to find her. The four of us marched right up to her. "Hello, girls," she greeted us with a smile. Thank goodness. We had caught her in a good mood.

"Hello, Mrs. Wainwright," we chorused all at once. Then there was dead silence.

Finally Stephanie cleared her throat. "Mrs. Wainwright . . . um . . . we were wondering if it would be all right to hang some posters up around school."

"We're having a dog wash at my house to earn some extra money," Lauren explained.

"Well, I don't see why not." Mrs. Wainwright looked down at us pleasantly.

"Great!" Stephanie started out the front doors. "Thanks, Mrs. Wainwright." We started to follow her — then remembered the bake sale.

We turned back and Patti cleared *her* throat. "We'd also like to have a bake sale after school one day."

"That sounds all right, as long as it doesn't interfere with classes. I may even buy something for my sweet tooth." This was a lot easier than we had expected! "Just be sure to let Mrs. Jamison know a couple of days ahead of time." Mrs. Jamison is the principal's secretary. She's nice to everyone.

"Thanks, Mrs. Wainwright," we said, and headed back for the doors.

"Let's get out of here before she changes her mind," Stephanie whispered.

Christy and Ginger were waiting outside for Christy's mom to pick her up. Ginger's mom works at the university, so sometimes Ginger goes home with Christy after school. They must have overheard us talking to Mrs. Wainwright. "Better get home,

Cinderellas," Ginger said snootily. "You've got to get to work."

Lauren was ready for them, though. "If we're Cinderella," she said, "I guess that makes you the ugly, wicked stepsisters." Christy and Ginger stuck their noses in the air and got into Mrs. Soames's car.

Pete Stone had overheard us, and gave Lauren the thumbs-up sign. "Way to go, Lauren." Pete's also in 5B. Sometimes he acts pretty weird, but most of the time we like him.

We unlocked our bikes from the rack and headed up Hillcrest toward Pine. "We'll have to get the poster board and markers out of my bedroom," Stephanie said as we turned into her driveway. "Then we can work in the apartment." Stephanie has a special playhouse in her backyard. When Mrs. Green was pregnant with the twins, she and Mr. Green had it built — they wanted Stephanie to have a place to go to when she needed some privacy. After all, for eleven years, she'd been the only child. Stephanie likes to call it her "apartment" because she thinks "playhouse" sounds too babyish.

We parked our bikes and walked into the Greens' kitchen. Mrs. Green was feeding one of the twins — I knew it was Jeremy because he had on blue overalls. To tell them apart, Mrs. Green dresses Jeremy in blue or green, and Emma always wears pink or red. Jeremy started wiggling and waving his arms when he saw Stephanie.

"Hi, girls." Mrs. Green smiled at us. "What are the Sleepover Friends up to this afternoon?"

We explained our dog-washing plan to her as she continued to try to get food into Jeremy's mouth. "A dollar fifty for miniatures, two fifty for mid-size dogs, and four dollars for large ones," Stephanie told her mother. This was the first time *I'd* heard anything about prices, but these seemed reasonable.

"Then we should get ten dollars for Bullwinkle!" I said dryly. Everyone laughed — including Jeremy.

Mrs. Green gave up on getting more squash into Jeremy and pulled him out of his high chair. He was a mess! It looked like most of the squash had ended up on his outside, instead of inside. Holding Jeremy at arm's length, Mrs. Green asked us, "How much would you charge to wash *him*?"

Chapter
4

We had decided to discuss our final schedule of projects at lunch that Friday. Stephanie was the last to arrive at the lunch table.

"What took you so long?" I asked. Wasn't she taking the trip as seriously as I was?

She pulled her chair in behind her. "I had to fix my French braid," she said nonchalantly.

"You did that all by yourself?" Lauren asked. "I didn't know you could do French braids. Will you teach me?"

"Yeah, I learned it from *Today's Teen*. There was a whole article on different kinds of braids," Stephanie said excitedly.

"I never got this month's issue of *Today's Teen*," Patti joined in. "Can I see yours, Stephanie?"

Was I the only one who cared about going to Wilderness World?

"You guys, we have more important things to think about than some magazine." I felt pretty irritated. "Can we get started now?"

Stephanie's eyebrows shot up. I knew what that meant. She thought I was being too bossy. But obviously someone had to take charge, or nothing would get done!

"Okay, okay," Stephanie said. "Guess what! I got us a window-washing job for a week from Saturday. And it pays *a lot.*"

"Way to go, Stephanie," I said. Maybe I wasn't giving her enough credit. "Where is it?"

"Over on River Drive," she explained. River Drive is one of the most expensive neighborhoods in Riverhurst, and the residents spend a fortune on their yards and houses. "The owner of the house is one of my dad's clients." Mr. Green is a lawyer with Blake, Binder, and Rosten.

"I can tell this project is going to be *very* profitable," Lauren said.

Patti nodded. "Yesterday, before the Quarks meeting started, I stopped by Mrs. Jamison's office and told her that we'll hold the bake sale on Monday of next week," she told us. Quarks is a club for kids who are really smart in science. "She promised she'd buy cookies for her grandchildren."

"With dog-washing at my house on Saturday, that makes three jobs we have lined up," Lauren said.

"Finding work is a lot easier than I thought it would be. We'll have enough money for the pass in no time."

"I've got some good news, too," I announced. "My mom talked to a couple of the women who volunteer with her at the hospital about our gardening services. A woman named Mrs. Levy wants us to come by a couple of days next week to weed and rake and stuff like that."

"How much will she pay us?" Stephanie asked.

"Mom didn't discuss a fee with her," I said. "But," I quickly added, "Bobby Kreiger mowed her lawn once, and she paid him twenty dollars." Bobby was in Mr. Keeler's class with me last year. He's a movie fanatic, too, so we got to be pretty good friends.

"Twenty dollars is good for just mowing a lawn." Stephanie was practically bouncing out of her chair. "At this rate, we'll be able to get *two* Wilderness World passes." I gave her a don't-get-carried-away look, but I was pretty excited myself.

We were so busy discussing our projects, we hadn't seen Jenny Carlin sit down next to us. Unfortunately, that didn't last long.

"Ew! Wilderness World," she shrieked. "Be sure you take plenty of bug spray. And watch out for poison ivy." Angela laughed on cue. I turned to look at them. They were both wearing *real* Hawaiian

37

flower leis around their necks! How dopey can you get? Brother!

I turned back to my friends without answering her. "What will they wear tomorrow?" I asked. "Grass skirts?" We all giggled.

Hope Lenski came over to our table and sat down beside Lauren. Hope's the newest girl in Mrs. Mead's class, and next to Patti, she's the nicest person I know. "You guys are so lucky you get to go to Wilderness World," she said, pulling out her lunch. She usually brings her lunch to school.

"Yeah, but it's going to be a lot of work," Lauren told her. "A four-day pass is really expensive. We each came up with an idea to earn money. Tomorrow we're having a dog wash at my house."

"I know. I saw the posters. They look great! I'll be sure to bring my dog, and I'll help spread the word," she volunteered.

"Thanks, Hope," I smiled.

During gym that afternoon, Henry Larkin and Jane Sykes also said their dogs needed to be washed. Judging from the response in Mrs. Mead's class alone, I had a feeling the dog wash would be a real success!

As soon as the three o'clock bell rang at the end of the day, the four of us ran out of class and hopped on our bikes. The sleepover that night was at Lauren's. We had a lot of organizing to get done before we fell asleep. "Let's meet right after dinner so we can concentrate on our plans," I suggested.

As Stephanie and I turned off at the corner of Hillcrest and Pine, I called to her, "My parents will come by to take you to Lauren's after dinner." Stephanie nodded and pedaled toward her house.

After my dad dropped us off at Lauren's house, her parents surprised us by offering to take us bowling at Bowl Riverhurst. The bowling alley had opened about a month ago. Everything was brand-new and automatic. You didn't even need to know how to keep score to play! It sounded like a lot of fun, but bowling was not on our schedule. As tempting as the offer was, I really wanted to say we didn't have time to go.

But Stephanie spoke up before I had the chance. "Neat," she said. "I've never been bowling before."

"I love bowling. I haven't been since we moved," Patti added enthusiastically. Lauren looked happy, too.

I didn't want everyone to think I was a drag, so I reluctantly agreed. "Sure." I tried to sound excited, but this change in plans was going to get us off schedule by at least two hours.

It seemed as though everyone in Riverhurst were at the bowling alley that night. Most of the kids were in high school. Mary Beth Young and Todd Schwartz were there. Todd lives across the street from Stephanie. He and Mary Beth have been dating for a while, but their relationship is on-again, off-again. I guess it was on that night. Even Lauren's brother Roger and his girlfriend Linda had gotten there before us. They saw us and waved.

"Hey, look!" Stephanie pointed at the snack bar. "It's Donald Foster." Yuck! Donald Foster lives next door to me. He is the second-most conceited guy in Riverhurst (after Taylor), but Stephanie thinks he's cute.

He turned around, caught Stephanie pointing, and immediately began walking toward us. One thing Donald can't resist is a captive audience. "Hi, girls," he smiled smugly.

"Hi, Donald," Stephanie said with a big smile on her face. "What are you doing?"

Donald thought awhile. I mean, how tough could the question be? "Bowling," he finally responded. Duh. No joke.

I figured I ought to get something out of having to stand there and watch Donald Foster flash his toothy grin, so I asked, "Are you bringing Lucky to our dog wash tomorrow?" Lucky is a collie who belongs to Donald's Aunt May. Aunt May lives about a half-mile away in Riverhurst, and sometimes she brings Lucky over when she stops by to see the Fosters.

"Sure," he said, turning to me. I immediately

40

regretted saying anything. I bet he thought I was on his list of admirers. "Where is it?"

"At my new house," Lauren interrupted. "On Brio Drive."

"Yeah, I know where that is. Catch you girls tomorrow morning," he winked at Patti as he went back to join his friends.

"What a hunk!" Stephanie said to Patti. Patti blushed and rolled her eyes.

Mr. and Mrs. Hunter motioned for us to join them at two adjoining lanes. "You girls can take the lane on the left." Mr. Hunter pointed. "We'll be right here next to you after we get some snacks for everyone." They headed for the snack bar.

We went to get bowling shoes and balls and returned to a shock more horrible than Donald Foster! Christy and Ginger were bowling in the lane right next to ours! Luckily, Ginger's parents were bowling with them, so they couldn't be too nasty.

"Oh, hello, girls," Christy said as she slipped her feet into her rented shoes. "Ginger and I are really looking forward to bringing Scamp to your dog wash." Scamp is Christy's terrier — and the last dog I'd hoped to see tomorrow.

"He likes to be *very* clean," Ginger added. "We'll be there to make sure you do a good job."

"Oh, good," Lauren said sarcastically under her breath. "Maybe we'll throw in some extra flea powder for you." I snorted with laughter.

Patti finished tying her shoes and jumped up to keep the argument from getting out of hand. She handed a ball to Lauren.

"Why don't you go first?" she suggested.

The rest of the game was relatively peaceful. Lauren bowled really well — she's pretty much a jock. I came in last, which didn't surprise anyone since I'm not athletic. And Stephanie actually won! She's got a good throwing arm but otherwise, she's no better at sports than I am. I guess having Christy and Ginger in the next lane brought out her competitive spirit. We obviously didn't have the same effect on them. The overhead electronic scoreboard showed that they each threw about ten gutter balls.

"Let's get out of here," Ginger said to her parents. Then she pretended to be talking to Christy but looked straight at us. "Now we know bowling is way uncool."

"Only if you're way bad," Lauren mumbled just loud enough for Christy and Ginger to hear. We all cracked up.

After our game was over, I checked the clock on the wall of the bowling alley. "I think we'd better leave, too, you guys," I said. "We've got at lot to do this evening."

As soon as we got back to Lauren's house, we went up to her room. I pulled my notebook out of my backpack. "I've made a schedule for our jobs," I said. I had figured out exactly what we needed to do to prepare for each job, and how long each thing should take. "We've already gotten behind, but if we work really hard, that won't matter." I could see Stephanie smirking. She always tells me I take things too seriously, but if I didn't organize us, we probably would never make it to Wilderness World. "From now on, though," I said, ignoring her, "we've got to stick to our schedule."

"I have a question," Stephanie said. "According to your schedule, when do we get to eat onion-soup-olives-bacon-bits-and-sour-cream dip?" That's Lauren's special recipe. She created it all by herself and has been perfecting it for about five years. *And* she's generous enough to still make it for us, even though she hardly eats it anymore.

"According to *my* schedule," Lauren answered, "now!" She led the way in the race to the kitchen to get the snacks together. I brought up the end. After all, I couldn't expect the Sleepover Friends to function without proper nourishment. Besides, I *had* scheduled a fifteen-minute break for snacks.

"What do we need for a dog wash, anyway?" Patti asked as she dropped ice cubes into four glasses. "I've never done this before." Patti's father is allergic to dogs, so they've never had one.

Lauren twisted the top off the Dr Pepper and

43

began to pour. "Shampoo . . . a hose . . . a brush to scrub with," she listed the supplies we'd need.

"And lots of towels," Stephanie added.

"Right," Lauren nodded.

I looked at the list I had made. "Do you still have that big metal washtub we used to play in?" I asked. "We can wash the smaller dogs in it." Lauren and I used it as a swimming pool in the Sleepover Twins days.

"Good idea," she grinned. "I think my father put it in the basement when we moved."

We left our chips and dip (plus Lauren's celery and carrot sticks) on the counter and filed down the basement steps to find the metal tub. It was easy to see that Lauren had inherited her messiness from her parents — the basement was a total disaster area. "Are you sure it's down here?" Patti asked meekly.

We hunted for the tub for almost forty-five minutes. Then Lauren stopped and froze like a statue. "Uh-oh," she finally said. "I just remembered . . . I think I saw my dad put the washtub in the garage."

"What?!" I fell in a heap on a pile of old lawn chair cushions. We were already *three* hours off schedule, and still hadn't gotten all of the equipment for the dog-washing together. Plus, I was exhausted, and we hadn't even really done anything yet!

We marched back up the steps and into the garage. Luckily, the washtub was in plain view. Right next to the tub was a stack of old buckets. "We'll probably need these, too," I said, scooping them up.

The shampoo, brush, and towels were a cinch to find since the Hunters keep them handy for Bullwinkle's baths. Now that we'd collected all of the supplies for the dog wash, we'd be prepared when the dogs started arriving in the morning.

We put all the stuff on the back patio and carried our snacks to Lauren's bedroom. Stephanie threw herself across the bed. "I can finally relax," she sighed.

"Not until we make the posters for the bake sale," I reminded her.

"Ugh!" Lauren groaned, taking a bite of rice cake with peanut butter. I tried not to watch. I think rice cakes taste like Styrofoam cups.

"Can't we make posters tomorrow?" Stephanie asked.

I was really getting frustrated. "You guys, if we don't get the posters hung up tomorrow, no one will come to the bake sale Monday. We have to make a profit from each job or we won't earn enough for the extra ticket to Wilderness World."

"Kate's right," Patti said. "She's gone to all this effort to take all of us. The least we can do is make it work."

"I guess we just thought it would be easier," Lauren said apologetically. She dug around in her

45

desk drawer for markers and construction paper. "Roger already said he'd hang up the bake sale fliers when he goes to Main Street tomorrow," she said. "And my mom's getting her hair cut at the mall. She'll ask them to put one on the bulletin board."

We all started scribbling away. Stephanie drew pictures of cakes, pies, and cookies, while the rest of us wrote the details. By the time all of the fliers were made, it was two o'clock in the morning. According to my schedule, we were supposed to have finished them by nine o'clock. We hadn't had time to do any of the regular Sleepover Friends activities like Truth or Dare or Mad Libs.

And for the first time in Sleepover Friends history, I had missed "Friday Night Chillers"! Every Friday night, Channel 21 shows two scary movies. I had already seen both of that night's features, but I still hated to miss them. After all, it was a sleepover tradition. I just hoped Wilderness World was worth what we were going through.

Chapter
5

That Saturday we all got up at seven o'clock. Even though we hadn't gotten much sleep, we were wide awake. Everyone was excited about our first job! Mr. Hunter fixed us whole wheat pancakes with fresh strawberries for breakfast.

The phone started ringing at eight — people wanted to make appointments to bring their dogs over. "It was a good idea to put Lauren's phone number on the posters," Patti said.

Lauren swallowed a mouthful of pancakes. "With these appointments *and* all the kids from school who said they'd bring their pets over," she said, "we should make lots of money."

"And don't forget the people we don't even know about yet," Stephanie reminded us.

"The best part of this job is that it doesn't cost *us* anything," I said, turning to Lauren. "Except for the shampoo. We'll pay your mom back when we're done." Lauren's mother had bought us a special pet salon shampoo. It was kind of expensive, but considering all the money we would probably make, it was worth pleasing the customers.

"Plus, it should be pretty easy. Nothing could be harder than washing Bullwinkle," Lauren laughed. "I've got tons of experience doing that."

By the time we finished breakfast and helped with the dishes, it was eight forty-five. According to my schedule, we were right on time. I looked at my notebook. "Let's go to your den and relax for a minute," I said. "We can figure out who's going to do what today."

"I'm definitely not going to wash any smelly old dogs," Stephanie said firmly.

"Why don't you fluff, Stephanie?" I suggested.

Her face lit up. "You mean *style* them after they're washed?" she asked. She has a way of making things sound more impressive than they actually are.

"Yeah, after they're dried . . . by me," I said. "I thought Lauren and Patti could wash." I looked over at them. Luckily, they didn't seem to mind washing. In fact, they were smiling.

When I checked my watch, it was already eight fifty-five! We had advertised that the dog wash opened at nine. "We'd better get started on Bullwinkle," I told them. "We want people to see we mean business."

"I put him out back before breakfast," Lauren said, opening the back door. When we stepped outside, though, Bullwinkle was nowhere to be found.

We looked around the backyard. Lauren's backyard is big, but so is Bullwinkle. If he were back there, we would have seen him. It didn't take us very long to figure out that he was missing.

"Maybe he ran away," Stephanie said with a concerned look on her face.

Lauren wasn't worried, though. "He's probably just sleeping somewhere. I'll look in the house," she said.

While Lauren hunted in the house, Patti and I set everything up in assembly line order: tub for washing, buckets for rinsing, towels for drying, and brush for styling. Stephanie walked back and forth screaming, "Bull-winkle!" at the top of her lungs. And she got more than she bargained for! Bullwinkle came bounding through the gate toward Stephanie — dragging Roger behind him!

"Heel, boy! Heel!" Roger yelled. But Bullwinkle's obedience school training wasn't exactly what you'd call a success. He ignored Roger and kept barking and running — straight for Stephanie! She just stood there, paralyzed with horror. She wasn't

49

scared of Bullwinkle — he never hurt anyone. But he has this bad habit. . . . Bullwinkle pounced on Stephanie, pinned her to the ground, and licked her face with his huge pink tongue.

Patti and I were laughing too hard to move. "Stephanie, the human lollipop," I said between gasps for breath. Luckily, Lauren had given up looking in the house and came outside — just in time! She ran over and helped Roger pull Bullwinkle off of Stephanie.

"Bullwinkle! Bad dog!" Lauren scolded. Bullwinkle whimpered and looked up at Lauren with sad puppy eyes. "Where *were* you two, anyway?" she asked Roger in an annoyed tone.

"I took him for a jog," Roger replied, equally annoyed. "I wanted him to get a little exercise before you girls turned him into Fifi the Wonder Dog."

Stephanie finally regained her ability to speak. "My hair. My nails. My *clothes*," she whimpered. "Donald Foster can't see me looking like this."

I had to admit — Stephanie did look a mess.

"After a couple of dogs, Stephanie, you'll look better than the rest of us," Patti reassured her. Either Patti didn't convince her or she didn't care because Stephanie continued to look depressed.

"Come on, you guys," I urged everyone. "Let's get started. People are going to arrive soon."

Lauren grabbed Bullwinkle's leash. He must

have known what we were up to because he didn't budge an inch. Patti helped Lauren pull, but Bullwinkle was a lot stronger — and fatter — than they were.

"Go get one of his treats, Kate," Lauren said between grunts and gasps.

I ran into Lauren's kitchen and grabbed the whole bag of treats. (Knowing Bullwinkle, one probably wouldn't be enough.) "Here, boy," I called, and held a treat over the tub of soapy water. What a mistake! Bullwinkle came charging toward me — right into the tub of water! A humongous wave splashed all over me. I still had the treat between my fingers, but Bullwinkle was one step ahead of me. He had his nose buried in the bag and was eating every last one.

"You were right, Patti," Stephanie was laughing, holding her sides. "Everyone else *will* look as bad as I do." I couldn't help laughing, myself. I must have looked pretty funny. Patti and Lauren finally got Bullwinkle to stand still long enough to hose him down and work the shampoo into a lather. Just in time. People from Lauren's neighborhood started arriving with their dogs. I grabbed my notebook and took down their names and any special instructions.

By the time Stephanie finished brushing Bullwinkle, we were already twenty minutes behind on our appointments. And people kept streaming into

51

the backyard. I was beginning to wish we hadn't done such a great job advertising. But I don't think I regretted it half as much as Stephanie did when Willie Judd walked through the gate! Willie lives down the street from Lauren, and Stephanie really likes him.

"Oh, no! I look awful! Patti, quick. Stand in front of me!" Stephanie frantically motioned for Patti to come to where she was standing. Patti's the tallest girl in the fifth grade, so I guess Stephanie thought she'd make a good shield from Willie. Unfortunately, it didn't work.

"Hi, you guys," Willie smiled and peeked around Patti's back. "Hi, Stephanie. I didn't know this was your dog wash." Stephanie stepped from behind Patti. "Oh . . . hi, Willie," she stammered. "This is actually for all of us." Stephanie was so embarrassed, she could hardly speak. She's ordinarily talkative and outgoing — but she usually hasn't just been pounced on by a 130-pound Newfoundland!

Willie escorted his dog to stand with the other pet owners.

"Maybe we should have the owners tie their dogs to the fence," Lauren whispered to me. "That way, we can take everyone in order."

"Good idea," I said. I organized all of the customers along Lauren's fence. Some people handed me the leash and said they'd come back and get their dog later. After each leash was securely fastened, I took my place on the assembly line. We tried to work quickly to make up for lost time.

For a while, everything ran smoothly. We worked on three dogs at a time. Patti and Lauren washed and rinsed one while I dried another and Stephanie brushed the third. Stephanie's part didn't take as long as the rest of us, so she was also in charge of collecting money and making change.

Around noon, Mrs. Hunter brought out a tray of tuna salad sandwiches and limeade for us, so we grabbed a few bites of lunch whenever we could.

A lot of kids from school showed up. Jane Sykes and Henry Larkin came pretty early. I knew Henry would, since he and Patti are an item. They sit next to each other in class. And Roger had spread the word around Riverhurst High, so a few people in his classes came. Even Tug Keeler brought his bulldog, Lump. Tug is the quarterback for the football team.

I was beginning to think nothing would go wrong. Boy, was I wrong! Just then, Ginger and Christy walked through the gate with Scamp. "Oh, hello," Stephanie greeted them coolly, proud that we appeared to be doing such a good job. "You can tie your mutt to the fence."

"Scamp is *not* a mutt," Ginger responded indignantly. "He's a purebred Jack Russell terrier. And, anyway, I have a twelve-fifteen appointment. I'm not waiting in that long line." She pointed to the five dogs along the fence.

I definitely would have remembered making an appointment for Ginger and her little rat. "You never told *us* about an appointment," I responded. "You'll have to wait — just like everyone else." I turned my back on her and knelt down to finish drying a basset hound.

Then Patti held my notebook in front of my face and pointed to Ginger's name — right next to "12:15." "They made the appointment with Mrs. Hunter while we were cleaning up the dishes this morning," she whispered. I looked up at Ginger. She had a smug expression on her face. Oh, well. The sooner we washed Scamp, the sooner they'd be out of our hair.

"Be sure to wash his paws really well," Ginger commanded. "And his ears are very tender. Don't get any soap in them." I was ready to soap Ginger!

Lauren, Patti, and I finished washing and drying Scamp pretty quickly. We were almost home free. The only thing left to do was for Stephanie to brush him out. But just as she started on his head, all the dogs suddenly began barking and howling. And before we knew what was happening, Scamp leapt out of Stephanie's grasp and headed through the Hunters' gate after a yellow ball of fur!

"Oh, no!" Lauren yelled. "The Lockharts' cat!" Christy jumped up and took off like a light after Scamp.

Ginger's face turned beet red. "You did this on purpose," she screamed at Stephanie. "There is no way I'm paying you one . . . red . . . cent!" She stormed out of the backyard.

We all looked at each other silently. Finally, Stephanie shrugged her shoulders and said, "Well, at least she didn't mention how awful we look." We burst into laughter.

"Look on the bright side," I added, winking at Lauren. "It doesn't look like Donald's going to show up." Lauren used to live on the other side of Donald, and she thinks he's as arrogant as I do.

"He must have gotten a better offer," she smirked.

Suddenly, I realized there was a commotion along the fence. All the dogs' leashes seemed to be in one big knot! I had tied them up too closely together, and they'd gotten so excited by the cat that they twisted up their leashes! Not only that, but some of the dogs we'd already washed were rolling around and playing in the dirt!

"Oh, no!" I shouted. "Where's my notebook?" I had to find out which dog was which, and get them back to their owners. "Has anyone seen my notebook?" Finally, I looked into the washtub and saw the blue cover resting at the bottom of the dirty water! All of the appointments were smeared. I couldn't read anything!

The best we could do was try to make all of the dogs presentable before their owners came back to get them. But where were we supposed to start? Some dogs needed to be washed *again*.

An English sheepdog dragged Lauren past me. "Look who it is!" she called as she flew by.

I looked in the direction she pointed. "Hope!" I shouted, trying to be heard over the racket. Hope and her five-year-old brother, Rain, walked through the gate with their dog. I had never been so relieved to see anyone in my life.

"What happened?" Hope asked.

"Don't ask," I said. "It's a long story, and we've got to get this mess in order before the owners come back."

"Rain and I will help," she offered.

"Thanks a lot, Hope," Patti said.

We unknotted the leashes and washed the dogs that hadn't been shampooed yet. Hope and Rain brushed out the dogs who had rolled in the dirt. They did such a good job, we didn't have to rewash them after all! By the time they were through, you couldn't even tell what had happened!

"You really saved us," I told Hope before she,

Rain, and Moonbeam went home. "I think we should pay you for all the work you did."

"You need your money for Wilderness World," she told me. "Besides, I love animals. I had a great time. See you on Monday." She smiled and waved good-bye.

After the last dog was picked up at about three o'clock, Patti, Stephanie, and I emptied and rinsed the buckets and washtub and put them back in the garage. Lauren gathered up all the soggy towels and went downstairs to stuff them in the washing machine. When she came back upstairs, we were all inside, lying flat on the family room floor.

"*Every* muscle in my body aches," I mumbled.

Lauren stretched out on the couch. "I never even knew I *had* so many muscles. I had no idea washing dogs could be such hard work," she said.

Stephanie pinched her nose. "*I* had no idea it could make you smell so bad," she said, sticking her tongue out. "P.U.!"

Patti lifted her head a little and looked at Lauren. "How much did we make, anyway?" she asked groggily.

"Yeah, did we make enough for the ticket to Wilderness World?" Stephanie asked hopefully.

Lauren mustered enough strength to push herself off the couch. She dumped the money out of her tennis-shoe box onto the coffee table and counted the cash. "Wow, you guys!" she exclaimed. "We made twenty-nine dollars and fifty cents!" We sat up when we heard the news.

"Excellent!" Stephanie cheered.

"After we pay Mom back the five fifty for the shampoo, we still have twenty-four dollars," Lauren calculated.

Mrs. Hunter peeked her head around the corner. "Congratulations, girls," she said. "This calls for a celebration. How about the Pizza Palace?"

"Yay!" we shouted. We forgot how tired we'd been just a little while ago.

"Roger can drive you home," Mrs. Hunter smiled. "We'll pick you up in about an hour and a half. That ought to be enough time to clean up."

The Pizza Palace has the best pizza in Riverhurst. We ordered a pizza with everything — except anchovies. Between the Hunters and the Sleepover Friends, we drank three pitchers of Dr Pepper.

I was so exhausted by the time I got back home, I fell into bed immediately. I had to rest for tomorrow. The next day, we were all going to meet at Patti's house to cook for the bake sale.

Chapter
6

I got up early Sunday morning to work on a new schedule, since I didn't have my job notebook anymore. On the last page of notes, I made columns to keep track of how much we had spent and earned. I recorded all the information from the dog wash.

Stephanie and I rode our bikes to Patti's together at nine-thirty. Lauren jogged over and was the last to arrive — as usual. "I'll tell my mom we're all here. She's working in the garden," Patti explained as she led us into her house. "She'll drive us to the Super-Save, and hang around in case we need help baking." The Super-Save is a huge supermarket. You can get all kinds of special ingredients there.

When Mrs. Jenkins came into the kitchen, her hair was pulled back in a bandanna and her face and clothes were covered with dirt. "Hi, girls," she said, smiling.

"Hi," we chimed back.

"I'll be ready to take you as soon as I wash up a little," she said, and went upstairs.

"While we're waiting to go shopping, let's decide what we're going to make for the bake sale tomorrow," I suggested.

"Sure," Patti agreed. "We can go into the family room."

We each found a spot on the floor. "I think we should bake four different kinds of desserts," Lauren said. "We could sell three types of cookies or brownies, and a cake."

"How about Mom's peanut-butter-chocolate-chip cookies, Kate's super-fudge, a pound cake, and some brownies?" Stephanie suggested.

Lauren rested her index finger against her chin and scrunched up her forehead. I knew that meant she was doing some serious calculations in her head. Finally, she looked at me. "How many pieces of super-fudge does your recipe make?" she asked. Super-fudge is my sleepover specialty. I've made it hundreds of times, so I didn't have to think about the answer at all.

"I make half a recipe for our sleepovers, and cut it into twenty-four pieces," I told her. "For the bake sale, though, we should make the whole recipe. We should get forty-eight pieces out of it."

"Perfect. One batch of super-fudge, two dozen brownies, four dozen peanut-butter-chocolate-chip cookies, and two pound cakes." Lauren rattled off the numbers.

Now that we'd figured out what we'd sell, we needed to make a list of ingredients so we'd be sure to get all the groceries in one shopping trip. "Patti, does your mother have a cookbook?" I asked. "We need a pound cake recipe."

"It's in the kitchen. I'll get it." Patti pushed herself off the floor and went into the kitchen.

"I know all the ingredients for the fudge, and we can just buy two boxes of brownie mix," I said, and recorded everything in my notebook. "Stephanie, do you know what your mother puts in her cookies?"

"I'd better know," Stephanie grinned. "I've watched her make it enough times!" Mrs. Green bakes a batch every time the sleepover is at Stephanie's house. Stephanie recited the ingredients while I wrote them all down.

Patti returned to the family room with her mother's cookbook. She plunked it onto the coffee table and opened it to the "cakes" section. "There are three kinds of pound cakes: fast-and-easy, chocolate, and Mrs. Baker's special pound cake."

"*Definitely* not chocolate," Stephanie said.

"We have enough chocolate already." Lauren and I nodded. Lauren peeked over Patti's shoulder at the page of recipes.

"Fast-and-easy. Mrs. Baker's has too many ingredients. We can save money this way," she said matter-of-factly.

"That's a good idea," I agreed. "Patti, what's in the recipe?"

By the time Patti named all the ingredients and I listed them in my notebook, Mrs. Jenkins had washed up. "Ready when you are, girls," she called.

It didn't take long to shop for the ingredients since we had written everything down. But when we heard the total cost, we were horrified! Lauren stared at the cashier. "Twenty-three dollars and twenty-three cents? Are you sure?" she asked. The cashier nodded.

"But that's almost all the money we earned from the dog wash!" Stephanie protested.

"It does seem like a lot, but I bet we'll earn it all back by the end of the sale," Patti assured us. I think she felt a little worried because the bake sale had been her idea.

Lauren hesitated, but handed the money to the woman behind the cash register. She only got seventy-seven cents back in change!

On the way back to Patti's house, though, we forgot all about the grocery bill. "*Everyone* will want to buy something," Stephanie said enthusiastically. "I told a bunch of kids who came to the dog wash about the bake sale, and they said they'd bring extra money on Monday."

"And Melissa said she'd spread the word in her class," I added.

By the time we pulled into the driveway, we were smiling at the thought of what a success the bake sale would be. "I'll be in the family room if you need me, girls," Patti's mom told us.

"Thanks, Mrs. Jenkins," I said.

"Do you think we should each mix up something different, or do everything together?" Stephanie asked as she grabbed a grocery bag and climbed out of the car.

"I think it'll probably be better organized if we all make one thing at a time," I said. "Let's start with the super-fudge, since it tastes better the longer it sits."

Lauren looked wistful. She loves my fudge, but she's only eaten one or two pieces since she's gone healthy on us. "Yeah, let's start with the super-fudge," she said sadly. "The super-fudge, which is full of sugar and bad for your teeth," she reminded herself softly. I grinned.

"Just remember — it's not to eat, it's to sell," I said cheerfully.

"*Someone's* got to sample it to make sure our

customers will be happy," Lauren said, looking almost hopeful.

"I will!" Stephanie and Patti said at the same time, and giggled.

"Well," I smiled, "maybe you're right." I looked at my watch. I couldn't believe it was already eleven-fifteen. "We'd better get started. Patti, can you find me a pot to cook this in? I'll also need you to grease a cake pan. Lauren, you'll need to pour the chocolate chips, and Stephanie will scoop the marshmallow fluff into the mixture when I'm ready," I directed them. I could practically make fudge with my eyes closed.

"Let's listen to some music while we cook," Stephanie suggested.

Patti turned the kitchen radio on. Then she handed me a pot for the fudge and began greasing a pan. I turned on the stove and started melting the butter. Lauren emptied the chocolate chips into the pot. We've had a lot of experience cooking together, so our system worked pretty well.

"I think this may be the best batch ever!" I smiled at the others as we scraped the last bits of chocolate off the sides of the pot and licked our fingers. We put the pan of fudge to one side to cool.

We started the pound cake next since that was the second hardest thing to make. Stephanie was measuring the sugar into a bowl when "Can't Wait

Till You Leave" by the Seven Wonders blared out of the radio. "Oh, I love this song!" she squealed, and started tapping her feet. She's a really good dancer and can't stand still when she hears music playing. She started spinning around in circles and throwing her head from side to side.

"I made up some new steps to go along with the chorus," she said, throwing both hands over her head. "Look!" We watched for a while, but went back to our stirring, measuring, and scooping. Stephanie kept going — she did a little hop to the right, then swung around with one arm strai — "Look out!" Lauren yelled. Patti and I looked up just in time to see Stephanie's hand swing by the counter and knock the bowl of sugar to the floor with a crash! Luckily, the bowl was plastic, so it didn't break — just bounced around awhile. But the sugar spilled everywhere!

Stephanie stopped dead in her tracks and stared at the mess. "Oh, you guys, I'm *really* sorry," she apologized.

"That's okay," Patti told her. "Sugar's something we definitely have a lot of." We had bought a whole five-pound bag — just in case.

Patti got a broom and dustpan out of the closet, and Stephanie helped her clean up the crunchy mess. I kept stirring the batter so it wouldn't get lumpy. "At least we have something to do while Kate stirs," Patti said grinning, trying to make Stephanie feel better.

Lauren greased a loaf pan. I poured the batter from the mixing bowl into the pan and slid it into the oven.

"It has to cook about forty-five minutes, so we can go ahead and mix up the brownies," I said. I read the instructions on the box of mix. All we had to do to make the brownies was add water, some vegetable oil, an egg, and nuts. "I don't think we could *possibly* mess this up," I said confidently.

Lauren started chopping nuts while Patti greased *another* pan. Stephanie mixed the brownies while I supervised and kept an eye on the clock. Just as she finished stirring in the nuts and pouring it into two square pans, the timer for the cake buzzed. My timing had worked perfectly! Lauren hopped up from her chair and pulled the cake out of the oven with a pot holder. "Now I know why they call it a pound cake," she said, pretending to heave the cake up onto the counter. "This thing could be used to work out with!"

"Is it supposed to be that heavy?" I asked.

"I guess so," Patti said doubtfully. "It *is* called a *pound* cake."

"I'm sure it's fine." Stephanie said confidently. "It *smells* okay. Now that everything's under control, why don't we take the timer with us and go watch some TV?"

"I don't think that's a good idea," I said. "We

should stay in the kitchen and keep our eye on every-thing. We can listen to the radio."

Soon the brownies were done, and we mixed up a second batch and put it in the oven. The kitchen felt like a steam bath, because the oven had been on for hours! After the first pan of brownies cooled, Patti started cutting them. "Uh, guys?" she said uncer-tainly. "Are all the nuts *supposed* to be on the bottom?"

"What?" I yelled, running over to look. So much for thinking nothing could go wrong! It was true. All the nuts had somehow sunk to the bottom of the pan and had crawled *underneath* the bottom layer. It looked awful!

"We can call them brownie upside-down de-lights," Patti said weakly. "No one will know the difference."

But I had a feeling everyone would figure out something went wrong. "Well," I said, checking my watch, "we've got to keep on schedule. We're ready to make the cookies and the second pound cake. This time, maybe Patti and Lauren should make the cake while Stephanie and I mix up the cookies. That way, we can trim some time off our E.T.F. — Esti-mated Time of Finishing," I said with a grin.

Since we'd already made the cake once, Patti and Lauren had no trouble the second time around. They were extra careful about measuring and mixing the ingredients. And Stephanie had watched her mother make the peanut-butter-chocolate-chip cookies as often as I'd made super-fudge, so the batter was ready in no time.

The cake and cookies had to be baked at different temperatures and we wanted to be sure to do everything right, so we set the cake batter aside and scooped teaspoonfuls of dough onto a cookie sheet. When the sheet was full, Patti set it on the oven rack and shut the oven door.

"What do you think we should charge for everything?" Stephanie asked.

Lauren had been thinking about that. "The fudge will probably sell best, so we have to be sure to charge enough. But the pieces are pretty small, so we can't be too greedy. I think twenty cents is fair. We can charge twenty-five cents for each piece of pound cake since the pieces will be pretty big, and fifteen cents each for the cookies and brownies."

"Sounds fair to me. Anyone for something to drink?" Patti asked.

"Yeah — I could use a glass of juice," I said. I was started to burn up in that hot kitchen.

"Coming right up," Patti said, opening the door of the fridge.

"Ew!" Stephanie wrinkled her nose. "What's that smell?"

Smell? "The cookies!" I screamed, lunging for the oven door. But not fast enough! A thin trickle of smoke was coming out the sides and when I opened the door, the cookies looked like little lumps of coal with chocolate chips in them. "We forgot to set the timer." Our eyes started to tear up, so Patti switched on the fan and opened a window.

"They're ru-ined!" Stephanie sounded like she was about to start crying.

"It's just one dozen," I said, trying to calm her down, even though I was upset, too. This was exactly the kind of thing that threw a schedule completely off track. "We'll just have to make the rest smaller to make up for these." We trimmed some of the dough off the cookies that were waiting to be put in the oven. After the smoke cleared a little, Lauren put them in to bake. Of course, we kept a careful eye on them to make sure they didn't burn. Finally, after three batches, all the cookies were done, and we put the second pound cake in for forty-five minutes.

It was almost dinnertime when we were finished stirring and baking that day. We had four dozen cookies, two pound cakes, two batches of brownies, and forty-four pieces of super-fudge. (We each had to sample the fudge. Even Lauren.)

Stephanie arranged the food artistically on plates. When she finished, she looked at the assortment and frowned. "It looks good, but it should look better," she said critically. "It has to look fantastic, so we'll sell every piece."

"I have an idea," Patti hopped out of her kitchen chair. "My mom has some doilies leftover from the last time we had guests. I know she wouldn't mind if we used them." We arranged the brownies and cakes on the doilies. They really did look a lot better.

"Oh, no!" I said, looking around. "Look at this mess. We still have at least another hour of cleaning up to do." Luckily I hadn't scheduled anything else for that day.

Patti handed us brooms, sponges, and a couple of rags. As we cleaned up we didn't have to worry about burning anything, so we talked and listened to the radio. "I think this is going to be great!" Stephanie exclaimed. "I bet we sell everything."

Lauren wiped the countertops with a soapy sponge. "I hope so," she said. "After all that money we spent on groceries, we need to sell every single thing to make a profit."

"Well, I'm sure it'll be a success," I said. "Everything looks terrific!" Patti looked up from loading the dishwasher and smiled.

By the time we finished washing the pots and pans and scrubbed the floor, countertops, and table, we were exhausted.

"I still have to do my math homework," Lauren

groaned. "Luckily, I don't have to take time to eat dinner. After smelling this stuff all day, I have zero appetite."

Patti, Stephanie, and I all opened our eyes wide, on cue. "What?" we screeched, looking at each other in disbelief. "Did we hear right? Lauren has no appetite???"

"Ha-ha," Lauren said as I pretended to take her temperature. "Very funny."

Of course, the rest of us hadn't done our math homework either since we'd been together almost the entire weekend. I didn't see how I'd be able to keep my eyes open long enough to finish it, though. And I was right. I went home and sacked out like a light.

After school the next day, the bake sale went pretty well. Mrs. Mead excused the four of us fifteen minutes before the three o'clock bell so we could get everything ready. Mr. Hathaway, the custodian, set up one of the lunchroom tables in the front lobby for us.

"Rats!" I said suddenly. "I wish we had remembered to buy a paper party tablecloth. It really would have given us a professional look."

"Oh, it looks okay the way it is," Patti said soothingly. "After all — it's just a student bake sale." I nodded grudgingly, but it's little details like that that really bug me. Anyway, I put index cards with the name and price of each item around the table. We had decided beforehand that Lauren was in charge of all the money.

Lots of kids stopped by before they got on their buses or bikes. Even some parents who were picking their kids up came in to buy the desserts. And Mrs. Wainwright and Mrs. Jamison stopped by — just like they said they would.

Practically everyone wanted the fudge and cookies — even if both were a little small. We also sold almost all of the brownies. No one seemed to mind the layer of nuts on the bottom. Jane Sykes thought they were so good, she even asked us for the recipe! Hardly anyone wanted the pound cake, though. And we found out why when Stephanie decided to sample it!

"Ew!" she cried, clutching her throat. "Get me some water, quick!" Patti ran to fill a paper cup at the water fountain, and Lauren and I crowded around to see what was wrong. After Stephanie gulped down the water, she held out her piece of cake and said, "You try it."

So I did — and instantly saw what she had been talking about! I quickly drank down the rest of her water. "I see what you mean," I said weakly.

"What's wrong?" Lauren demanded.

"Well," I said, looking at Stephanie, who was

starting to have a guilty expression on her face, "re-member when a certain someone — I won't mention any names — accidentally spilled all the sugar on the floor?" Lauren and Patti nodded. I raised my eyebrow and continued, "Did anyone remember to measure out more sugar to put in the cake?" Lauren gasped and put her hand over her mouth. Stephanie looked down at her red sneakers. Patti just stared at me.

Then Lauren started giggling. "So, it's pretty tasteless, huh?"

I nodded. "Not very sweet," I concluded. "But maybe it's perfect for your sugar-free diet," I said as Patti and even Stephanie started to crack up. "No thanks!" Lauren snickered. At least *one* pound cake had come out okay.

Jenny and Angela stopped by the table as we were packing up the leftovers. Jenny picked up two brownies that hadn't been wrapped yet. She handed one to her sidekick and took a bite herself. "This isn't the best brownie I've ever tasted," she complained. "But here's my contribution to the Wild West trip." She plunked thirty cents into our shoebox.

"Wilderness World," Stephanie said through gritted teeth.

Ginger and Christy walked by on their way out the door. They must have overheard, because Ginger said, "*You* know, Jenny, didn't you go there when you were little?" They hooted as they walked away.

We cleaned everything up and rode our bikes to my house. Lauren counted all the money. "We made thirteen dollars and thirty cents," she announced.

"Hmm," I frowned.

"That's not as much as I thought we'd make," Patti said with a worried look.

"Well, we didn't sell quite everything," Lauren said thoughtfully. "And after all, we spent twenty-three dollars and twenty-three cents on groceries." She did some quick mental calculations. "So we have fourteen dollars and seven cents total," Lauren said.

I couldn't believe it! After the dog wash and an entire Sunday of baking and cleaning up, we only had fourteen dollars and seven cents? We were all pretty worried — especially me. It would be tough to take another job *and* do the ones we'd already arranged. I was really beginning to think that the Sleepover Friends weren't going to make it to Wilderness World after all. And we'd already worked so hard!

Chapter
7

Monday night was the first time the Sleepover Friends had had a chance to relax since Thursday. Before we split up, we agreed to ride our bikes over to clean Mrs. Levy's yard immediately after school on Tuesday. Patti was even going to miss a Quarks meeting — the supreme sacrifce.

"She has all the tools, so we won't have to buy anything," I said. Lauren breathed a loud sigh of relief. We were pretty discouraged from the results of the bake sale.

On Tuesday we bounced back from our defeat. At lunchtime we talked about how fast and easy the yard work would be, and how we were sure to have our money in no time. I really wanted to cheer Patti up, because she felt responsible for coming up with the bake sale idea. But we assured her it wasn't her fault — it wasn't anyone's fault.

Mrs. Mead devoted the two hours after lunch to oral reports on current events projects. Luckily, the four of us had each given ours the week before. Each student was supposed to limit the presentation to ten minutes, but Karla Stamos droned on for half an hour. In addition to being *really* boring, she's a real grind. I thought the bell would never ring. When it finally did, we raced out of our desks to the bike rack.

"I'll be able to stay the entire time since Roger and I traded chores," Lauren said as she hopped on her three-speed.

Patti pedaled up the hill on Hillcrest with hardly any effort. "It was nice of Roger to switch days with you," she said.

Lauren laughed. "He said it was worth getting a vacation from the Sleepover Friends for four days over spring break!"

Stephanie changed the subject. "Did you notice the new shade of fingernail polish my mother bought me?" She flashed a neatly manicured hand at us. "It's called Really Red."

I couldn't believe it! She'd painted her nails to pull weeds! "Stephanie," I said, "why did you fix your nails when you knew they'd get ruined?"

"After that embarrassment on Saturday with Willie Judd, I wasn't about to take any chances," she said.

"Mrs. Levy is a widow and lives alone," I told

her. "The chances that Willie will wander into her yard are slim, at best."

But Stephanie wasn't persuaded. "You never know. I always like to be prepared."

"This ought to be a snap!" I predicted as we rounded the corner to Mrs. Levy's street. "How bad can it be?"

Mrs. Levy's house was the second one on the right. We definitely couldn't have missed it. It was set back pretty far, and the front yard looked like it hadn't been raked since 1980! The rosebushes along the front fence were knotted with overgrown weeds. Plus, my mother had told me Mrs. Levy wanted some flower beds dug in the backyard. From the looks of things, I didn't think we had to worry about earning money for Wilderness World anymore. We'd still be cleaning Mrs. Levy's yard during spring break!

I was afraid to look at the others. Suddenly, I understood how Patti felt about the bake sale. "I guess I'll go tell Mrs. Levy we're here," I muttered. I slithered off my bike and walked to the front porch. Mrs. Levy must have seen us pull into the driveway because she opened the door before I even knocked.

"I'm so glad you girls could help me out," she smiled warmly. "I want to get my garden started, but I can't do all the preparations myself. I'm not as young as I used to be."

I introduced myself and the others. Then Mrs.

Levy explained everything she wanted us to do and led us to the shed to show us the gardening tools.

"If you have any questions or need anything, I'll be right in the house," she told us. "Please don't hesitate to come ask." She went back inside.

"We'd better get started," Lauren said, trying to be cheerful. "We'll never make it to Wilderness World just standing here." Groaning inwardly to myself, I picked up a rake and headed back to the front yard.

Mrs. Levy watched us from the window almost the whole time. Occasionally, she'd come out and explain that she wanted something done a particular way. We'd all helped our parents out with gardening — except maybe Stephanie — so we knew pretty much what we were doing.

Mrs. Levy only had two rakes, so while Patti and I raked the front yard, Lauren and Stephanie pulled out the weeds around the rosebushes. After we'd worked about an hour, Mrs. Levy raised the window and called, "Would you girls like to come in for some Oreos and milk?" We dropped our tools and practically *ran* into the house. I had definitely worked up an appetite.

After our break, Stephanie said she was tired of bending down all the time, and my hands were sore from raking, so we switched jobs. Since we had to get home for dinner, we left at five-thirty, after we had put all the tools away neatly in the shed. I told Mrs. Levy we'd be back the next day to finish.

Lauren and Patti pedaled ahead. They didn't seem to be tired at all. But Stephanie and I were miserable. "I think I'm starting to get calluses on my hands," Stephanie complained.

"If that's the worst of it, you're lucky," I told her. "I can tell I'm going to have a huge blister by tomorrow." I could hardly hold the handlebars on my bike.

"Why didn't you two wear gloves like Patti and me?" Lauren asked.

Stephanie and I looked at each other. "Gloves?" we said at the same time.

Lauren let us catch up to her. "Yeah, didn't you notice? There were a few pairs of gardening gloves in the shed," she said. "I figured you saw them and just didn't want to wear them."

Now I felt even worse! I let out a long, exasperated sigh.

On Wednesday, Mrs. Mead gave us a spelling test first thing. I had been so tired after cleaning Mrs. Levy's yard the night before, I'd completely forgotten about the test. Plus, I could barely read my own handwriting. I didn't have any blisters, but my hands were still really sore. It hurt just to hold a pencil. After the test, we traded papers with other kids in the class to grade them.

I did worse than usual — a seventy-nine. Stephanie and Lauren usually do the same in just about every subject, so they both got eighties. Neither one was happy, but they hadn't studied, so they didn't expect to do well. But poor Patti! She always gets *A's* in spelling — in everything, for that matter.

"An eighty-seven!" she exclaimed. "I haven't done this badly in spelling in my life! I hope this t-r-i-p to Wilderness World doesn't make me f-l-u-n-k!'"

The rest of the day was filmstrips, lectures, and more oral reports. We really didn't have to concentrate — or write — very much. Thank goodness! I was so worn out, I fell asleep twice during the filmstrips, and only woke up when my elbow slipped off my desk!

After school, we dragged ourselves to Mrs. Levy's house, less enthusiastic this time. "I'll be glad when all of this is over," Stephanie said tiredly. "My nails are *ruined*. And I guess I can kiss my jeans goodbye. I'll never get the grass stains out!"

"I'd just like to get one good night's rest," I agreed.

"At least we're earning money," Lauren pointed out. "And it isn't costing us anything."

I'd forgotten how much we had left to do until we pulled into Mrs. Levy's driveway. Patti looked at the mounds of raked leaves that still needed to be bagged. "Gosh, look at all those piles," she mumbled.

Once we got started, the afternoon actually went pretty well — mostly because I remembered to wear a pair of gloves. So did Stephanie. Once we got all the leaves bagged and finished weeding around the rosebushes, the yard looked a lot better.

"Oh, no!" Stephanie exclaimed suddenly.

"What happened? Did you break a nail?" I teased.

Stephanie smirked at me. "No, but I have to get home. It's already five o'clock. One of my dad's clients is coming for dinner, and I promised my mom I'd help her get ready."

I had no idea it had gotten so late. Feeling a little defeated, I put my rake back in the shed. "We won't be able to finish this evening anyway," I told Lauren and Patti. "We'll just have to come back tomorrow. Lauren, can you get Roger to do your chores again tomorrow afternoon?"

"Probably. He's got a lot riding on this trip, too," she smiled wearily.

When I got home that evening, I tried to figure out how we could be sure to get all the work in Mrs. Levy's yard completed before dinner on Thursday.

The only thing I could think of was to hire a couple more people to help us. Asking Melissa and one of her friends was a possibility. But they were only eight years old — how much help would they be? And they'd need supervision. Mrs. Levy was only paying us twenty-five dollars, and we couldn't afford to split it with anyone else. After the bake sale disaster, we needed every cent for ourselves!

The bike ride to school the next day was really quiet. We were more interested in staying awake than anything else. The yard work was even starting to get to Patti and Lauren. By the time we got to school, I needed toothpicks to keep my eyes open. I had stayed up late the night before trying to catch up on all the reading assignments I hadn't done — just in case Mrs. Mead decided to give a pop quiz. It was no use, though. I'd finally given up because I kept falling asleep on my desk.

At lunch, Jane Sykes asked Stephanie why she looked so pale and tired.

"Are you doing some kind of science experiment to see how long you can go without sleeping or something?" Pete Stone asked.

"Yes, that's right, Pete," I answered sharply. "We thought it would be *fun* to be totally exhausted." I didn't mean to sound so snippy — after all, Pete probably meant well. But this rigorous schedule was starting to make me irritable.

"Don't be silly, Pete," Jenny giggled. "No one would look that hideous on purpose." She and Angela broke into fits of laughter. I glared at them.

I didn't know what to expect that afternoon when we got to Mrs. Levy's, since it had rained after we left the night before. I really wasn't sure how much we'd still have to do to satisfy Mrs. Levy.

But when we got to Mrs. Levy's driveway, I was actually pretty relieved. The front yard was completely finished. There wasn't a single weed around the rosebushes.

"Wow! This looks great!" Lauren exclaimed.

"Yeah, we don't have much work left at all," Stephanie said, sounding more cheerful.

Then Patti pedaled her bike past the house into the backyard. "Uh-oh," she said as she stopped and turned to face us. "Look at what the rain did to our flower beds!"

Lauren, Stephanie, and I pushed our bikes up to where Patti was standing.

"Gross!" Stephanie exclaimed. "It's a good thing I was about to give this sweatshirt away."

The backyard looked like one big mud puddle! The rain had made all the flower beds we'd dug the day before run together.

"Well . . . the sooner we get started, the sooner we'll be done," I told them.

As usual, Mrs. Levy watched us from the window. Around four-thirty, she brought out a tray of snacks and told us to come in and rest if we got tired. We really wanted to get the job over with, though, so we kept on working.

Putting the mud back where it belonged was pretty easy since we each had a shovel to use. But it was kind of tough maneuvering around the puddles and slippery spots. We were all getting tired and bored — especially Stephanie.

The final straw was when she lost her grip on her shovel, slipped, and slid on her stomach from one end of the flower bed to the other!

We all stood in shocked silence, waiting for the explosion. "It's a good thing you like to wear black, Stephanie," I said nervously, "because you're *really* wearing it now!"

Patti helped Stephanie up and managed to get only a little of the mud on herself. Stephanie was actually a good sport about the catastrophe. "Mud-packs make excellent facials," she declared through the coat of slime.

"Way to go, Steph," Lauren said, and patted her back.

By five o'clock, the mud that wasn't on Stephanie was back where it belonged. Before we told Mrs. Levy we were leaving, we stood back and admired our work. "I think we should go into the yard-cleaning business," Stephanie said proudly. "We could call it Sleepover Friends Lawn Styling, Inc."

"It's catchy," I giggled. "But what about your fingernails?"

"Oh, no big deal," she shrugged. Lauren, Patti, and I rolled our eyes and smiled at each other. She was so unpredictable!

Mrs. Levy came out of the house to say good-bye. "Thank you girls so much," she said. "You did a super job. Anytime you want to come by and pick some flowers, feel free." And, in addition to the twenty-five dollars we were supposed to get, she gave us a five-dollar bonus!

"Wow, thanks, Mrs. Levy!" Stephanie said as she held the crisp five-dollar-bill in her hand. "If you ever need help with your yard, just give us a call!" Obviously she'd forgotten all about the blue jeans and sweatshirts this job had ruined.

Mrs. Levy walked us to the end of the driveway and waved good-bye as we quickly pedaled away. "Bye. Thanks," I called back to her. Three jobs down, one to go!

Chapter
8

"Pass me the avocado dip, please," Patti asked. Lauren stuck her tortilla chip in one last time before surrendering the bowl to Patti. I guess tortilla chips aren't too bad for your teeth.

The sleepover was at Stephanie's that Friday, and we were all lying on the red-and-black rug in her apartment.

"We finally have a night when we don't have to be thinking about Wilderness World," Stephanie said happily. Lauren nodded and drank a swig of diet Dr Pepper to wash down her last bite of chip and dip.

"We're not home free yet," I reminded them. "We made a lot of money yesterday, but we still need a lot more to be able to pay for a four-day pass to Wilderness World."

"Well, we've already earned forty-four dollars

and seven cents," Lauren said. "And we have the window-washing job tomorrow."

"What if the window-washing doesn't pay enough?" I asked.

"Uh . . . you guys?" Stephanie began.

"Stephanie already told us they'd pay *a lot*," Lauren interrupted. "Right, Stephanie?"

"Uh . . . yeah . . . right," Stephanie murmured. She looked kind of nervous but didn't say anything. I guess she was as worried as I was that "a lot" wouldn't be *enough*. After all, the next day was Saturday, and we were supposed to leave on Monday. That left only Sunday to make up the difference between what we earned and what we'd still need.

I'd been doing some thinking. "Well, if we *don't* have enough money by Monday, I've decided I won't go, either," I announced. "I'll just stay at Lauren's house over spring break. Melissa can use the tickets to take three of her friends. All for one and one for all."

Patti smiled wistfully at me. "That's really sweet of you, Kate. But we couldn't let you do that, right, guys?" When Lauren and Stephanie didn't say anything, she continued, "I've already decided that if we don't get the money, *I* won't go. I'll use the time to catch up on my grades."

"Wait a minute," Lauren said suddenly. "I think I should be the one to stay home, since . . . since

. . ." She couldn't even think of a reason!

"No, no, it should be me!" cried Stephanie. "I spilled the sugar and I — "

"You what?" I asked.

"Nothing," she mumbled.

Well, this was great, I thought. Just great. If we kept up like this, *none* of us would go! I looked around at their three glum faces. They really wanted to go on this trip. I couldn't blame them. So did I. We'd worked so hard the past week.

Even though all of us were pretty sad, I *really* felt sorry for Stephanie. She's usually so bubbly and talkative — especially when the sleepover is at her house. But she hardly said a word all night. And she almost *never* bites her nails, since she likes for them to look perfect. By the time we fell asleep, she'd nibbled on them so much she barely had any nails left!

I didn't know what to do. If the window-washing job didn't pay well enough, how would we find a job before Monday that would? I had a suspicion that none of us would get to go to Wilderness World the next week.

"Rise and shine, girls! Wipe that sleep out of your eyes," said Mr. Green. He had warned us the night before that he'd be waking us early so we'd be sure to have time to get ready and ride our bikes to River Drive.

Stephanie rolled off her fold-out mattress. "I haven't been able to sleep late for over a week," she said, rubbing her eyes. "I'm going to get bags if I don't get some rest *soon!*"

The grueling schedule was getting to me, too. "I can't wait until this is all over and we're all on Wilderness World's Lion Tamer," I said, trying to sound more positive than I felt. The Lion Tamer is the longest roller coaster in our area. It has three loops, including one that's all the way upside down.

"In a few hours, we'll be finished earning the money we need," Lauren said, determined to be enthusiastic. "Then we'll have an entire day to relax and decide what rides we want to go on first!" Patti and I nodded, but Stephanie just shrugged. Her attitude had really changed. When I first won the passes, she had acted the most excited about the trip. But for the past two days, whenever anyone else talked about it, she had acted weird.

I switched on the TV while we all dressed in our work clothes. Wendy Kraft, our local weatherperson, was reporting the forecast. "Turn it up," Stephanie said. "I need to know if it's going to rain." She's always worried about rain since her hair frizzes whenever there's rain or snow or something like that.

I turned the volume up with the remote control. "Breezy this morning, getting up to about seventy degrees in the city by this afternoon. That's about ten degrees higher than average temperature for this time of year," Wendy said.

"Whew — dress light, you guys," warned Lauren.

After we changed, Mrs. Green made us omelets and fruit salad for breakfast. Mr. Green gave us the address of the house we were supposed to report to and the name of the owners — the Lyonses. I carefully wrote it all down in my notebook.

We each made a roast beef sandwich from the Greens' dinner leftovers and packed up a bag lunch to take with us.

"We'd better get going," I said when everyone was ready. "We don't want to make a bad impression by being late."

"Right!" Lauren nodded.

We rode our bikes to the Lyonses' house. When we got to the right street number, we skidded to a halt and stared. The Lyonses lived in a very modern house. It was pretty big. And it was made almost completely out of glass!

"All right!" Lauren exclaimed, trying to look on the bright side. "This ought to pay for the rest of the ticket and more! Way to go, Stephanie!" She turned to smile at Stephanie, but Stephanie was looking at the ground and kicking the dirt around with her feet. Lauren raised her eyebrows, looked at me, and shrugged.

"We're not going to get *any* money until we're finished," I reminded Lauren. "Let's get started!"

Stephanie led the way to the front door and rang the doorbell. A tall woman in a jogging suit answered the door. "Hello, girls," she smiled, then she looked at Stephanie. "You must be Ron Green's daughter." Stephanie does look a lot like her dad. They have the same dark wavy hair and round face.

"Yes," Stephanie answered politely. "And these are my friends — Lauren, Kate, and Patti." We each nodded and smiled when she introduced us. I stood up as tall as I could (okay, so that's not very tall!) and tried to look professional.

"You're a little younger than I imagined," Mrs. Lyons said as she led us around to the back of the house. "Do you think you can handle such a big job?"

"Oh, sure," I said airily. "No problem."

At the back of the house was a patio and a swimming pool. Mrs. Lyons pointed to a pile of supplies and said, "I've set everything you'll need over here." There was an array of buckets, rags, paper towels, bottles of glass cleaner, and squeegees. There was also a pile of old sheets to protect the plants in front of the windows. There were two ladders on top of the sheets. Everything was all set up. We wouldn't have to do anything except clean.

"If you need me for *anything,* feel free to come get us. Mr. Lyons and I will be playing tennis until lunchtime," Mrs. Lyons said, pointing further back. I hadn't even seen the tennis court — it was sort of hidden behind a row of hedges. Wow, these people must be really rich, I thought. I bet they're paying us a *fortune*.

"Thanks," we grinned as Mrs. Lyons picked up her tennis racket and headed toward the court.

"Well," I clapped my hands. "Let's decide who's going to do what."

Patti and Lauren volunteered to do everything above their heads as high as they could reach, while Stephanie and I, since we're short, would get up on the ladders and do the tops of the windows.

We got started. It was easy for Lauren and Patti to reach pretty high, since the handles on the squee-gees were so long. But we still had to work pretty hard — and it was starting to get really warm in the sun.

It wasn't long before our arms were shaking from reaching up, and we had emptied our buckets what seemed like a million times. I was aching all over, and Stephanie looked like she didn't feel much better. At noon, we decided to take a lunch break. We took our brown bag lunches under a shady tree in the front yard.

"Phew!" Patti said. "Remind me not to pursue this as a career!" Lauren and I laughed, but Stephanie hardly cracked a smile. Come to think of it, she had hardly said a word all morning. What was wrong with her?

I guess Lauren was thinking the same thing, because she tapped her sneaker against Stephanie's and said, "Hey, Steph, what's up? Don't tell me — you'd rather be shopping?" Patti and I grinned, but Stephanie remained glum. Lauren shrugged her shoulders and let the subject drop.

After we finished our lunches, we reluctantly went back to work. At least there was a breeze blowing, and it kept my bangs from sticking to my forehead. The backs of our T-shirts stuck to us with sweat. I tried to think about the big muscles I was building, but what use would big muscles be if I died of exhaustion, right here on the Lyonses' lawn?

By mid-afternoon, we were ready to clean the windows at the front of the house. We were doing a pretty good job, if I do say so myself. Mrs. Lyons had come by to check up on us once or twice, and had smiled approvingly. Once she even brought us a pitcher of lemonade. It didn't take us long to gulp it down.

Then I offered to let Lauren be up on the ladder and me on the ground, to give Lauren's arm a break. I just wanted a change of pace. Patti and Stephanie switched, too.

Just as I dipped my squeegee and reached up for the highest spot, I heard a voice bellowing behind me, "Well, if it isn't Cinderella and her three dwarfs!" When I turned around, Taylor Sprouse, Andy Hersh, and a couple of other guys from sixth grade were standing on the sidewalk, laughing.

"You're mixing up your fairy tales, dumbo," Patti retorted. Taylor didn't seem to understand that the joke was on him. He just laughed and skateboarded down the street. None of us thought twice about the incident after he was gone. We had much more important things to think about — like how we were ever going to finish washing these dumb windows!

The sun seemed to get hotter and hotter the longer we worked. For the last couple of hours, we worked it out so that three people worked while one rested. We also coordinated it so that two people used the squeegees while the third person went over everything with a rag. One good thing about the hot sun that day was that we could really see what a great job we'd done!

Just as the sun started to go down, I was finishing up our last panel of living room windows. "I think this looks really great!" I called down from my ladder. "And just think — this time Monday, we'll all be at Wilderness World!"

"Yay!" Lauren and Patti cheered beneath me.

Stephanie had been sitting in the shade under a huge willow tree in the yard. "Uh . . . you guys," she stammered. That was just about the first time she'd spoken since lunch. "I have to tell you something." I stopped moving the squeegee back and forth and turned to face her. "We're only getting fifteen dollars for this job."

"What?!" I shrieked, almost losing my balance completely!

"I thought we were being paid by the hour!" Lauren said.

"I never told you *that,*" Stephanie defended herself. She was right. We had never bothered to ask her how much we'd be getting. We had just assumed we'd be paid by the hour. "Besides, it seemed like so much money when my dad told me about it."

No wonder she had looked so nervous every time we mentioned money! She'd known all along there was no way to earn enough for the trip. I was really angry with Stephanie, but I also felt sorry for her. After all, none of our projects had been absolutely flawless — not even mine.

But now what were we going to do? Even Patti looked panic-stricken.

"When we're done, let's go to my house and count everything," Lauren said grimly. "Maybe we've forgotten something. And then we'll know what the story is."

I quickly cleaned the last pane of glass.

Mrs. Lyons came out as we were stacking up the equipment. "You girls did a wonderful job today. Mr. Lyons and I have never had *anyone*, not even professionals, wash the windows so well."

Then why don't you pay us more money, I pleaded with her silently. Apparently my ESP skills haven't improved any — she gave us only the fifteen dollars she had promised. More proof that ESP is just mumbo-jumbo, as far as I'm concerned.

We all climbed onto our bikes and slowly rode up the hill toward Lauren's house.

"My arms are killing me," Stephanie said quietly.

Lauren said, "Remind me next time we do this to wear rubber gloves. My fingers are going to look like prunes *permanently*."

"There definitely won't be a *next time* for me," I announced. "My days of window-washing are over!"

Chapter
9

We rode our bikes to Lauren's house and went into the kitchen. Mrs. Hunter came in and said, "How did it go, girls?"

"Don't ask," Lauren groaned. She poured out four huge glasses of diet Dr Pepper, and fixed us a tray of apples, pretzels, and dried apricots. She saw the expression on my face and said, "Kate, this will give us new energy, without causing our blood sugar levels to crash in an hour." I caught Patti's eye and rolled my eyes. Give me barbecue potato chips any day!

We went up to Lauren's room and crashed on the floor.

Lauren swept the clutter from the top of her desk onto the floor. She bent over and pulled our money box out from under her bed and dumped the cash onto the desk. I got my notebook out of my pocket, ready to record any important information. Lauren counted the money and frowned. "If we add the fifteen dollars we earned today, we've still only got fifty-nine dollars and seven cents," she said.

"I just don't see how that's possible," argued Stephanie. It seems like we've made a lot of money from all of our jobs."

It was incredibly depressing to realize how little money we'd made after so much effort.

"The bottom line is that we still need almost thirty dollars," Lauren said.

I groaned. Thirty dollars was a lot of money! And we only had *one day* to get it!

"What are we going to do?" Patti said softly.

"We could try asking our parents for it — split four ways it would only be about seven dollars and fifty cents per family," Lauren suggested.

"I don't think so," Stephanie said. "They made it pretty clear that we needed to come up with the money ourselves." She had a point.

"But what could we possibly do to earn thirty dollars in one day?" I asked. No one said anything for a really long time.

"Maybe our parents would *pay* us money for doing special chores around the house," Patti suggested. "That way it wouldn't be *giving* us the money."

"My parents already include my chores as part

of my allowance, and I spent all I had," Lauren said.

"We already did our spring cleaning," Stephanie added. "There's nothing big left for us to do at my house."

Patti hung her head and nodded. We were all really bummed.

"Oh, it's all my fault!" Stephanie cried. "I never should have taken that dumb window-washing job."

"No, it's mine," I interrupted her. "I should have planned this out better."

"You guys, it's not anyone's fault," Patti broke in.

Lauren looked at the pile of cash on her desk. "Patti's right. Right now we have to think of something we can do to earn the money. Or all our work will have been for nothing," she said.

"Um . . . could we figure this out over some more Dr Pepper?" Stephanie asked.

Down in the kitchen, Lauren broke down and started searching the cabinets for chips. Now I *knew* she was down! I think everybody was pretty sure my parents — and Melissa — would be going to Wilderness World without us.

We were standing around, sipping our drinks sadly, when Roger came in through the back door. He lives in an "apartment" over the Hunters' garage, in the backyard.

"Hey, squirt," he said, ruffling Lauren's hair.

She hates it when he does that, but now she just smoothed it back down absentmindedly. Roger got something to drink, then I guess he noticed that we were standing around like a bunch of mummies.

"Why do you guys look so upset?" he asked, gulping down some milk.

"We've got a problem," Lauren said morosely.

"Yeah, we probably won't be going to Wilderness World after all," I explained. "We still need thirty dollars, and it's already Saturday night — too late to find another job."

"Gee, that's too bad," Roger said sympathetically. "But I thought you had it worked out so that you'd be able to earn enough by now."

So Lauren told Roger about the bake sale and the gardening and the window-washing. Suddenly her eyes lit up like a Christmas tree.

"Roger, could *you* please lend us the money?" she begged. "I promise I'll pay you back as soon as I can."

We all stared at Roger while he thought about Lauren's suggestion. "Uh, um, gee. That's a lot of money," he said. "And how fast could you pay me back, anyway?"

Our heads all drooped again. It had been a great idea. Just then Mr. Hunter came into the kitchen. "Oh, there you are, Roger. I just wanted to remind you of all the things you have to do around the house tomorrow. You know what your mother said — if your room isn't spick-and-span by the time we get home tomorrow, no camping trip next week." Roger's face clouded over. "Oh, hi, girls," Mr. Hunter said, as if he were just seeing us for the first time. He smiled cheerfully and left.

Roger was frowning. "This is the last thing I need! I promised Linda we'd go on a picnic tomorrow," he muttered. I looked over at Lauren and was surprised by the expression on her face. Her eyes were positively gleaming. The only time I'd seen her look like that was when she had a chocolate-chocolate-chip ice-cream cake for her birthday.

"So, Roger," she said casually. "Sounds like you've got a busy day tomorrow." She blew on her nails and rubbed them on her T-shirt.

"Yeah, so?" Roger said grumpily.

"So how badly do you want to go on your camping trip?" Lauren asked mischievously. "Bad enough to pay us to do your stuff tomorrow?"

Roger turned around to look at her. Patti, Stephanie, and I turned to look at her. Then Roger cracked a big smile, and he and Lauren met in the middle of the kitchen to do a big high-five. "You're on!" he yelled.

"Yay!" Patti, Lauren, Stephanie, and I jumped

up and down. We were going! Thanks to Roger, the Sleepover Friends would actually be spending spring break in Wilderness World!

The phone rang at nine-thirty Saturday night. I picked up the phone on the first ring. I'd been waiting all evening for Lauren to call and fill me in on the details that she and Roger had worked out. "Hello?" I said.

"Kate, it's me," Lauren answered excitedly. "Roger and I have figured it all out." She went on to explain how we were going to do Roger's chores without their parents finding out. We were sure that Mr. and Mrs. Hunter wouldn't be thrilled about us doing Roger's work. But since they were leaving early the next morning to visit some friends who lived a couple of hours away . . . As soon as they pulled out of the driveway, Lauren would call Patti, Stephanie, and me to say it was okay to come over. Then Roger would leave to go on his picnic with Linda. The plan was absolutely foolproof!

Sunday morning everything went exactly as planned. Patti, Stephanie, and I met at our usual corner and rode our bikes over to Lauren's. When we got there, Roger had a list of chores ready for us. He gave it to Lauren and waved good-bye to us happily.

Lauren read the list out loud. "Clean his apartment, wash and iron his shirts, straighten out his closet, polish his loafers . . ." It went on and on.

"What?!" Stephanie protested. "He expects us to do all that?!"

"I had no idea he wanted us to do all this stuff," Lauren apologized. "I thought it was his regular household chores."

Just as I was about to suggest we refuse to do anything on the list, Patti spoke up. "It's not really fair," she agreed, "but we don't have a choice. If we don't do this for Roger, how will we earn the extra money?" Unfortunately, Patti was right. We couldn't really complain.

We went up to his "apartment" and surveyed the job ahead of us. It wasn't pretty. I knew it would be bad. He *is* a Hunter, after all. But I was totally unprepared for what I saw! I thought Lauren's room was something, but it didn't hold a candle to Roger's!

His clean clothes were piled on his bed, his desk, and his chair. His dirty clothes were in a disgusting heap in back of his bathroom door. I don't even want to talk about the bathroom. And I couldn't tell if he had a carpet or not: he had wall-to-wall books and newspapers.

"I didn't know we'd need to bring tools for this job!" Stephanie exclaimed. "Like a shovel!"

103

"Ugh!" I groaned. How could anyone live like this?

"Well, let's get going," said Lauren grimly. "Grab the laundry basket." We piled the basket high and Lauren and Patti took it down to the Hunters' basement, where their washer and dryer were. Lauren took an armful of clothes and shoved whatever would fit into the washing machine. She didn't even bother to sort them. After all, he said to clean, but he never specified *how*. Then she dumped a cupful of detergent into the top and closed the lid. "We'll just use cold water for everything," she said. "That way, nothing will get messed up."

Then we started on his room.

"Uh, guys," I said innocently as we stood there trying to decide what to tackle first, "do you think we should be wearing surgical gloves to prevent contamination?" Stephanie and Patti almost fell over laughing, and Lauren pretended to threaten me with Roger's baseball bat. Then we got serious. While Stephanie dusted everything in the room and vacuumed his carpet, I straightened up Roger's drawers and bookshelves. I was completely grossed out when I found a moldy bologna sandwich behind an old biology book! Yuck! Lauren put his clean clothes away and straightened his closet. She found shoes in there that he hadn't worn since seventh grade!

"What time is it? I'm hungry," Lauren announced. That certainly wasn't a news bulletin to the rest of us! "Let's grab something to eat. We'll need energy for this afternoon." That was fine with me — though I sure didn't want a bologna sandwich!

After lunch, we took turns checking on the laundry. All in all, we had done *four* humongous loads! Most of the stuff came out all right, but in the load I took out, all of the T-shirts Roger wore to track practice were pink!

"I guess it wasn't such a good idea to wash these with red sweatpants," I said sarcastically.

"Oh, well," Lauren grinned. "I hear pink is very 'in' this year."

"It is according to Jenny Carlin!" Stephanie giggled.

As the clothes finished drying, Patti ironed Roger's shirts. "He'd better switch to permanent press!" she moaned.

Still, everything seemed to be under control. . . . Stephanie, Lauren, and I were putting the finishing touches on Roger's room when all of a sudden we heard Patti yelling, "Oh, no! Bullwinkle, come back here!" At the sound of Bullwinkle's name, Lauren dropped Roger's loafers and raced out of his room. Stephanie and I followed her.

When we ran through the kitchen door, we saw the tip of Bullwinkle's tail as he disappeared into the living room — with a pink T-shirt on his head and a pair of pants on his tail! And Patti was right behind him! "He knocked over the laundry basket!" she screamed. "And I had ironed and folded everything neatly!" She's usually calm, but you wouldn't have known it if you'd seen her trying to catch that runaway Newfoundland!

The four of us finally managed to corner Bullwinkle in the bathroom. Luckily, we saved the clean clothes Bullwinkle was wearing before he could do any damage. As Lauren said, "Roger won't even notice a paw print or two."

Around five-thirty we had finally finished everything on the list. We stood in the middle of Roger's room and looked around us with satisfaction. "I don't think this room has been this clean since before he moved in here," Lauren said.

"We did a good job," Stephanie said proudly. "We really earned that money!"

All Patti said was, "I'm glad Horace is only six years old."

We went back into the big house and washed our hands and faces. Then Lauren treated us all to some of her mom's neat hand lotion — it smelled like almonds. "There's no way I can save my hands at this point," Stephanie mourned.

"Try not to think about it," I advised. But my hands felt like sandpaper, too.

"Just think, once we're at Wilderness World, we

won't have any chores or jobs or anything for four days!" Patti exclaimed happily. We all smiled. The Sleepover Friends were unstoppable!

We went down into the kitchen and made about a hundred bacon-lettuce-and-tomato sandwiches for dinner. Being Roger's personal slaves had really made us hungry!

I carried the plate of sandwiches to the family room, Lauren was in charge of drinks, and Patti and Stephanie looked through the cabinets and refrigerator and found chips and leftover potato salad. After I set the plate down, I switched on the TV. A black-and-white Linda Rogers and Terence McMillan film was only about half over. "Oh, great!" I said. "This is one of my favorite old movies."

"Can't we watch something else — like *Dance Craze?*" Stephanie asked. "You've seen this movie tons of times."

"But — " I began.

"There you guys are!" Roger interrupted, coming through the door. "Why are you goofing off? Did you get everything done?"

Lauren's eyes narrowed to little slits. She and Roger usually get along really well, but she was fed up with all the demeaning tasks he had given us. Patti, Stephanie, and I all watched to see what would happen. "Roger, we're through being your servants," Lauren said angrily. "We're off duty."

"Did you polish my loafers?" he asked.

"Yes," Lauren said through gritted teeth.

"Clean my room? Organize my closet?"

"Yes. Yes."

"Iron my shirts?"

Patti stood up. "Yes!" she said firmly. Roger looked up in surprise. He had never seen Patti's aggressive side — hardly anyone has. It usually only comes out when she's being protective of Horace or something.

Now Roger looked pretty taken aback as he met Patti's blazing eyes. "Oh, okay," he said uncertainly, as she stood in front of him with her arms folded. I guess she had really hated ironing those shirts! "Uh, well, that's great, guys. I'm, uh, sure you did a great job." He actually started to back up a little! Then he fumbled for his wallet. "Uh, here you go — thirty dollars, like we agreed. Is that okay?"

Patti took the money, folded it, and stuck it in her jeans pocket. "That's fine," she said tightly. "Thank you."

"Yeah, thanks, Roger," Stephanie and I chorused.

After Roger had left the room, still looking at Patti strangely, we burst into hysterical laughter.

"Patti! That was so great! I've never seen Roger look so worried!" Lauren gasped, wiping tears away from her eyes.

"Yeah!" I agreed. "Leave it to Patti, the Tiger Lady!" Patti blushed and looked down, and suddenly she was just good old Patti again.

We sat down and devoured the rest of the sandwiches. Then we watched TV for a while. I meant to get my stuff together and go home to give my parents the good news, but the truth is, we must have all fallen asleep! The relief of finally having enough money for Wilderness World must have caught up with all of us. I could hardly keep my eyes open, so there was no way I could muster enough strength to ride my bike home!

When Mr. and Mrs. Hunter came home, they found our worn-out bodies strewn across the family room. I was sacked out in front of the TV, which I had been too tired to turn off. Lauren was stretched out full-length on the couch. Patti and Stephanie were each curled up on chairs.

"Goodness — George, look at this. Why do you think they're so tired?" Mrs. Hunter's whisper sort of woke me up. "It's not even seven-thirty. And they finished all their Wilderness World jobs yesterday."

I tried my hardest not to smile. I didn't want them to know I was listening. They had no idea we'd spent the day working for Roger — until he came whistling into the kitchen wearing one of his newly pressed shirts, a tie we'd uncovered in the wreckage, and a pair of freshly polished shoes!

"Well, look at you!" Mrs. Hunter said. "Don't you look spiffy."

"Hi, Mom and Dad," Roger greeted his parents innocently.

"Hi, Roger. What did you do all day?" Mrs. Hunter asked.

"Oh, this and that. You know," Roger responded vaguely.

"It looks like you've been busy washing and ironing," Mr. Hunter said, raising an eyebrow at his wife.

"Huh? . . . oh . . . yeah," Roger said without thinking.

"And did you get your room clean, son?" Mr. Hunter asked.

"Yeah, sure. What'd you expect?" Roger bluffed.

At this point, the four of us decided to "wake up," and started sitting up and stretching. "Hi, Mrs. Hunter," I said groggily.

"Hi, girls. How come you're so beat? Did you do something fun today?"

We just looked at each other and groaned. Patti was looking under the couch for her other sneaker when we heard Mr. Hunter come in through the back door. "Ann," he called, "come and take a look at this."

We froze. Roger froze, too, and his eyes got big.

Mrs. Hunter went out the back door and we heard her climb the stairs to Roger's room.

We sat there holding our breath until the Hunters came back into the family room. "How could one person have done all that in one afternoon?" Mrs. Hunter asked Roger.

Roger couldn't take it. He turned to his mother with the same expression on his face that Bullwinkle has just after he's done something especially bad. "Okay, okay," he said, looking down at his shoes. "I confess. I paid Lauren and her friends to do all my work. They needed the money."

"But I don't understand," Mr. Hunter said, turning to us. "Why did you still need money? You worked all week to earn your ticket."

"Our plan only worked halfway," I explained. "We had some unexpected expenses. . . ."

"Some project failures . . ." Patti continued.

"I'm so proud of you girls," Mrs. Hunter beamed. "You've really learned about earning money and hard work."

"And honesty," Mr. Hunter added as he glanced sideways at Roger. "I think this calls for a bonus." He handed us each a new five-dollar bill!

"Excellent!" Stephanie shouted as Lauren, Patti, and I jumped up and down and thanked Mr. Hunter.

"Wilderness World, here we come!" we shouted. We were actually going to make it!

Chapter
10

Monday morning, we were all ready at the crack of dawn for the Wilderness World trip. Sunday night, the four of us had called each other to find out what everyone was going to wear for the ride to the park. We decided on T-shirts and shorts. Stephanie was wearing black and red, of course, Patti was wearing blue, and I was wearing yellow. I also decided to wear my new vest and high-tops.

"I'm going to wear pink," Lauren told me. "Roger gave me all the T-shirts we ruined yesterday! I've got a whole new wardrobe now!"

We had to leave early since it takes about five hours to get to Wilderness World. I was so excited I woke up way ahead of schedule and had two hours to get ready! When I went to the kitchen to fix myself some cereal I found Melissa, already dressed and sitting at the table munching on a doughnut. And boy, did she look excited!

Melissa held her doughnut out. "Hi, Kate!" she practically yelled. "Want a bite?" Melissa *never* shares her doughnuts. She really was in a good mood!

I reached for the box of Cracklin' Day cereal. "No, thanks. Where are Mom and Dad?" I asked.

"They're in the garage loading up the mini . . ." she said, then stopped suddenly and put her hand over her mouth.

I couldn't believe my ears! "The what?"

"Oops! It was supposed to be a surprise."

I threw open the door to the garage. Sure enough! Mom and Dad were standing next to a brand-new, bright red minivan!

"Surprise, honey!" my dad said.

"How did you get this without my finding out?" I asked.

"Oh, that was the easy part," my mother explained. "You've hardly been home lately. Your dad and I picked it out on Saturday and brought it home last night."

"Unfortunately, my sports car wasn't really practical anymore, so we traded it in," my father said. "It was the end of an era."

Melissa joined us in the garage. "I picked out the color!" she said excitedly. "Right, Daddy?"

"Yes, and you did a great job helping us surprise

Kate," he smiled. Melissa grinned proudly and hugged my father.

My parents had asked Lauren's, Patti's, and Stephanie's parents to bring them over at eight o'clock. Everyone was right on time — even Lauren! Nobody wanted to be late for Wilderness World. You should have seen the looks on their faces when they saw the new van!

"Awesome!" Stephanie shouted. "That's a great color."

"It's really cool, Kate. But I can't believe you kept it a secret from us!" Lauren said.

"I just found out about it this morning," I defended myself. "Anyway, wait till you see all the stuff inside!"

Stephanie asked her mom to take a picture of all the Sleepover Friends in front of the new van. After that was done, Lauren, Patti, and Stephanie hugged their parents good-bye. Stephanie also gave Jeremy and Emma butterfly kisses on their cheeks and they laughed.

"Did you remember to pack your toothbrush, honey?" Mrs. Hunter asked Lauren.

"Yes, Mom," Lauren rolled her eyes. "I remembered everything." I could tell she was really embarrassed and was ready to get going. So was I!

"Let's get in the van," I suggested. "I'll show you what I brought for the trip!"

Our parents chatted a little while longer, which gave us plenty of time to talk about the next four days and to explore the van.

"This is so cool!" Stephanie said excitedly. "What a great tape deck! And six speakers! There's so much room, we could practically *dance* in here!" Uh-oh! I wasn't sure if the van was really equipped for Stephanie's enthusiastic style of dancing!

"*And* a sun roof," Patti added, turning the crank to open it a little.

"Melissa will sit up front with my parents, so we can each have our own window," I pointed out.

After the excitement of the new van wore off a little, Stephanie grabbed a bunch of magazines out of her book bag. "I brought all the new issues for us to read," she said. "*Star Turns, Teen Topics, Today's Teen,* and *Beauty Book*. And . . . guess who's on the cover of *Heart Throbs*! Kevin DeSpain!" We all squealed. He may not be a great actor, but he's definitely a heartthrob!

I showed them the games that Melissa and I usually play on long car trips — magnetic checkers and electronic soccer. Plus, I had bought a new book of Mad Libs, just for the occasion.

Patti held up a library book. "Look what I brought to read at night — with the Wilderness World theme in mind, of course," she announced. She turned the cover so we could all see the title —

The Adventures of Clarence Percy, Forest Ranger.
"Plus, my backpack's full of snacks — cheese pop-corn, tortilla chips, barbecue corn chips. . . . Five hours can be a long time if you don't have proper nourishment." We all laughed.

"I brought stuff, too," Lauren said, and we all groaned loudly. She pretended to hit us with her knapsack.

"Any food's fine with me, as long as we don't have to bake it!" I said.

Lauren pulled her camera out of her backpack. "Sit together. I want to get a picture of everyone," she said.

"I brought the video camera, too. We won't be able to take it on the rough rides, of course, but we can use it at night in the cabin, or in the Johnny Appleseed Arboretum," I told the others.

Finally we were ready to head to Wilderness World. My dad started the van up. "No school for a week!" Lauren shouted as we pulled out of the driveway onto Pine Street.

"Yay!" we all cheered.

At first, we were so excited and there were so many magazines, games, and food, that the time passed pretty quickly. We even filled up almost half the book of Mad Libs! Melissa needed to stop to go to the bathroom once, so we all got out to walk around a little and buy some soda. I don't remember much after that, though. We were still so tired from our busy week that we fell asleep for the last hour and a half of the trip!

Melissa was more than happy to wake us up. "We're here!" she yelled. "We're really here!"

"Already?" Stephanie asked groggily. But she came to life when she looked up and saw a larger-than-life-sized grizzly bear staring at her from the parking lot entrance! It wasn't real, though. It was a mechanical bear that moved its arms and head and talked.

"Neato!" Lauren's eyes opened wide.

My father talked into the speaker in the bear's stomach, and "the bear" directed us to our cabin. A large bearded man dressed in a forest ranger uniform met us at our cabin door.

"It must be Clarence Percy," Stephanie whispered.

"Hi, I'm Clyde Rogers," he said. "I'm so glad you all could make it to Wilderness World. My! You have an awfully big family!" he chuckled and his large belly bounced up and down.

"Oh, they're not all ours," my dad laughed. "They're the Sleepover Friends!" We poked each other and giggled.

A photographer from the park took a couple of pictures of me shaking Mr. Rogers' hand, me with my parents and Melissa, and all of the Sleepover

Friends together. What if they used the picture of the four of us together in their advertisements? That would show Taylor, Jenny, Christy, and Ginger!

Our cabin was really cool. It was made out of real logs. And the bathtub was made out of tin — just like the ones the settlers used. Thank goodness the cabin wasn't completely old-fashioned, though! We *did* have a TV. There were two bedrooms with two double beds in each. Mom, Dad, and Melissa put all their stuff in one room so we could have the other one all to ourselves. We unpacked our suitcases quickly since we wanted to get on as many rides as possible.

I had already given my parents the money we earned for the extra pass, so while we unpacked, my father bought it. He handed us each a ticket. "Don't lose it. After all your hard work last week, I don't think any of you will want to sit in a cabin for four days," he said.

"No way," I shouted as I headed for the door.

"Meet us at the Fireside Restaurant for dinner in three hours, okay?" Mom called behind us.

"Okay," we yelled, and raced toward the park entrance. We each grabbed a brochure with a description of all the rides and hurried through the gate. Then we each headed in a different direction.

"Hey, hold on, you guys!" I said. "We've got

to get organized. Now, where are we going to go first?"

Everyone spoke at once. Patti wanted to go to the Mississippi River Water Journey. Stephanie suggested we do something that wouldn't make us too hot and tired — like the Tom Sawyer Treehouse. Of course, Lauren really wanted to go through the Everglades Survival Trail since it would be adventurous.

I was beginning to think earning the money for the trip was the easy part! "We're going to be here for four days," I said. "We'll be able to do *all* those things. Let's just pick one thing and do it." I looked down at my brochure and one ride really caught my eye. "Like the Lumberjack."

No one was willing to give in. We each wanted our own choice to be the first ride of the trip. We argued for a while over what to do first, and I was getting frustrated that we were wasting so much time. Then a sudden movement caught my eye, and I looked around to see the Paul Bunyan Gift Shop. Then I stared! I couldn't believe my eyes! I didn't need my glasses to see who was in there.

I turned back to the others. "I see something more interesting than any ride," I grinned and pointed to the gift shop, where Christy Soames and Ginger Kinkaid were huddled behind the door, excitedly looking at postcards!

Patti's mouth dropped wide open, and Lauren scrunched her face up as if she were really angry. "I don't believe them!" she said.

"At least we know where we're going first now," Stephanie said slyly.

"Right!" the rest of us agreed.

The four of us ran over to the shop. We snuck up behind Ginger and Christy until we were practically breathing down their necks. Then Lauren leaned way over Ginger's shoulder.

"Hello," she said calmly. They whirled around and were so surprised to see us they almost jumped out of their skins! "I didn't realize preschoolers had spring break this week, too," Lauren said snootily.

"Very funny, Lauren Hunter," Ginger huffed. Her face was so red you could hardly see her freckles!

"So, this is your dad's idea of a really cool vacation, eh, Christy?" I chortled. "I'm glad to see someone in your family knows what's hot and what's not."

"It's your fault we're here!" Ginger snapped.

"My dad read about your winning the passes in the *Riverhurst Clarion*," Christy explained. "He surprised us with tickets this morning. If I had known before today, I would have told him we didn't want to come here."

"It looked to me like you were having a pretty

good time." Lauren pointed to the postcards in their hands.

"Oh — shut up!" Ginger said, and they stalked away with their noses in the air.

"It doesn't really matter to me what ride we go on now. Nothing could be as much fun as telling off those two," Stephanie said, laughing.

The four of us put our arms around each other. It had been a lot of work to get here, but it was worth it! Sleepover Friends, forever!

#35 The New Stephanie

"I can't believe it," Kate said, rolling on the floor with laughter. "Stephanie, you failed the niceness quiz! It's incredible! It's impossible!"

"I don't see what's so funny," I snapped. "You wouldn't be laughing if *you* failed the quiz. How come you guys all came out nice, and I came out insensitive?"

"You probably just didn't understand the questions," Patti said reassuringly. "A lot of them were tricky."

"I've had enough!" I practically shouted. "I'm hungry and I'm going to the kitchen for more fudge."

"You're kidding. Ten minutes ago you said you were stuffed," Lauren reminded me.

"I changed my mind! A girl's allowed to change her mind, isn't she? Especially," I added sarcastically, "if she's as snobby and self-centered as me."

SLEEPOVER FRIENDS™
by Susan Saunders

Available wherever you buy books...or use this order form.

THE BABY-SITTERS CLUB®

Collect Them All!

by Ann M. Martin

The seven girls at Stoneybrook Middle School get into all kinds of adventures...with school, boys, and, of course, baby-sitting!

For a complete listing of all the Baby-sitter Club titles write to:
Customer Service at the address below.

Available wherever you buy books...or use this order form.

Scholastic Inc., P.O. Box 7502, 2931 E. McCarty Street, Jefferson City, MO 65102

Please send me the books I have checked above. I am enclosing $ _____
(please add $2.00 to cover shipping and handling). Send check or money order — no cash or C.O.D.s please.

Name _____

Address _____

City _____ State/Zip_____

Please allow four to six weeks for delivery. Offer good in U.S.A. only. Sorry, mail orders are not available to residents of Canada. Prices subject to change.   BSC790